A BATTLE OF LOVE

The butler then announced,

"The Marquis of Darincourt, my Lady."

The Marquis was not surprised that Charlotte was obviously waiting for him.

She turned round from the window where she was standing to hurry towards him.

She held out her hand and he kissed it gracefully before he began,

"You look very beautiful, Charlotte, and I think that you know why I have come here to see you this afternoon."

He felt that he was being slightly precipitate.

At the same time it seemed unnecessary to utter a number of unimportant words before coming to the point.

To his surprise Charlotte took her hand from his.

She turned away to walk towards the mantelpiece.

As she did so, the Marquis could see the perfection of her figure and the graceful way she moved.

He followed behind her slowly and, on reaching the fireplace, Charlotte turned round to face him.

The Marquis realised that she was behaving a little strangely and he asked her,

"What is troubling you? You don't seem as pleased to see me as I had hoped."

"I have something to tell you."

He thought that her voice seemed a little uneasy.

THE BARBARA CARTLAND PINK COLLECTION

Titles in this series

A BATTLE OF LOVE

BARBARA CARTLAND

Barbaracartland.com Ltd

THE BARBARA CARTLAND PINK COLLECTION

Dame Barbara Cartland is still regarded as the most prolific bestselling author in the history of the world.

In her lifetime she was frequently in the Guinness Book of Records for writing more books than any other living author.

Her most amazing literary feat was to double her output from 10 books a year to over 20 books a year when she was 77 to meet the huge demand.

She went on writing continuously at this rate for 20 years and wrote her very last book at the age of 97, thus completing an incredible 400 books between the ages of 77 and 97.

Her publishers finally could not keep up with this phenomenal output, so at her death in 2000 she left behind an amazing 160 unpublished manuscripts, something that no other author has ever achieved.

Barbara's son, Ian McCorquodale, together with his daughter Iona, felt that it was their sacred duty to publish all these titles for Barbara's millions of admirers all over the world who so love her wonderful romances.

So in 2004 they started publishing the 160 brand new Barbara Cartlands as *The Barbara Cartland Pink Collection*, as Barbara's favourite colour was always pink – and yet more pink!

The Barbara Cartland Pink Collection is published monthly exclusively by Barbaracartland.com and the books are numbered in sequence from 1 to 160.

Enjoy receiving a brand new Barbara Cartland book each month by taking out an annual subscription to the Pink Collection, or purchase the books individually.

The Pink Collection is available from the Barbara Cartland website www.barbaracartland.com via mail order and through all good bookshops.

In addition Ian and Iona are proud to announce that The Barbara Cartland Pink Collection is now available in ebook format as from Valentine's Day 2011.

For more information, please contact us at:

Barbaracartland.com Ltd.
Camfield Place
Hatfield
Hertfordshire AL9 6JE
United Kingdom

Telephone: +44 (0)1707 642629
Fax: +44 (0)1707 663041
Email: info@barbaracartland.com

THE LATE DAME BARBARA CARTLAND

Barbara Cartland who sadly died in May 2000 at the age of nearly 99 was the world's most famous romantic novelist who wrote 723 books in her lifetime with worldwide sales of over 1 billion copies and her books were translated into 36 different languages.

As well as romantic novels, she wrote historical biographies, 6 autobiographies, theatrical plays, books of advice on life, love, vitamins and cookery. She also found time to be a political speaker and television and radio personality.

She wrote her first book at the age of 21 and this was called *Jigsaw*. It became an immediate bestseller and sold 100,000 copies in hardback and was translated into 6 different languages. She wrote continuously throughout her life, writing bestsellers for an astonishing 76 years. Her books have always been immensely popular in the United States, where in 1976 her current books were at numbers 1 & 2 in the B. Dalton bestsellers list, a feat never achieved before or since by any author.

Barbara Cartland became a legend in her own lifetime and will be best remembered for her wonderful romantic novels, so loved by her millions of readers throughout the world.

Her books will always be treasured for their moral message, her pure and innocent heroines, her good looking and dashing heroes and above all her belief that the power of love is more important than anything else in everyone's life.

"Love is always with you. Love never leaves you. From the highest mountain to the bowels of the earth love is always at your side.

And in your many lives yet to come love will always be following you."

Barbara Cartland

CHAPTER ONE
1819

The Marquis of Darincourt drove his phaeton with a flourish out of London.

He was well aware that every pedestrian he passed stopped and stared as he flashed past them.

The two horses that he had purchased at Tattersall's Salerooms were superb and matched each other perfectly.

The special phaeton, that he had designed himself, was yellow with black wheels and quite the smartest one in the whole of St James's Street.

The Marquis himself was well worth looking at too.

He was very handsome and in his looks and in his behaviour he lived up to his nickname, which was 'Darin the Daring'.

He had earned it when he was plain Captain Clive Darin in the Army.

He would undertake any mission however difficult and risky and yet he had succeeded in remaining alive.

The Marquis was today setting off on what was to him a new mission.

It was unlike anything that he had done before.

He had decided to be married.

He had been aware ever since the War was over, and he was moving around as one of the more celebrated

1

bachelors in the whole of the *Beau Monde,* that he would eventually have to take a wife.

He himself had been an only son.

He was well aware that his father before he died and all his relations had been terrified that he would be killed on the battlefield.

He had thought to himself at the time that he would have to marry as it would be a great pity if the Darincourt name, which had played its part in British history all down the ages, should come to an end.

The Marquisate, which had been created a hundred years before, was an additional glory and it was something which should not be lost.

The Marquis was well aware of the importance of his position, his great wealth and his good looks.

It meant that there was not a *debutante* who was not striving to attract his attention or an ambitious Mama who was not praying that he would become her son-in-law.

It had not made him conceited, just slightly cynical.

He felt at the back of his mind he would like to be married for himself rather than for his possessions and his contemporaries would laugh at him for being sentimental.

At the same time he was an avid reader.

He had therefore often thought that he would like to search for true love as it had been sought for in the past.

He had been very impressed by the poems written by Lord Byron.

He, of course, knew him as they both belonged to the same Club, which was White's in St. James's.

The Marquis on his return from the War to England then spent a considerable amount of time with exceedingly attractive and sophisticated married women.

They were only too willing to receive him secretly when their husbands were away in the country.

They were definitely of the *Beau Monde* and yet the Marquis found that they behaved like the French *cocottes* he had known in Paris.

That was while he was in France with the Army of Occupation.

Now not only his grandmother but several of his relations were begging him, almost on their knees, to take a wife.

He had looked at the *debutantes* and thought that he had discovered a perfect pearl amongst them.

Lady Charlotte Warde was the only daughter of the Earl of Langwarde and was most undoubtedly the greatest beauty of the younger generation.

She had been a top *debutante* the previous year and Lady Charlotte had received, the Marquis was told, dozens of proposals of marriage.

Almost every eligible bachelor had laid his heart at her feet and she had refused them all.

It meant, the Marquis had supposed, that she was waiting to fall in love.

He had first met Lady Charlotte Warde at a ball.

When he had danced with her, he thought that her great beauty was even more outstanding than it had been described to him.

She had almost classic features. Her skin was as white as marble and soft as a rose petal.

She was very sure of herself and therefore amusing and fun and she was not too shy occasionally to utter a *double entendre* or a provocative reply to a question.

By the third time the Marquis met her there was no doubt in his mind that she would grace the end of the table at Darincourt Hall and would also undoubtedly be the most beautiful Peeress at the Opening of Parliament.

He danced with her at several other balls.

They daringly sat out in the garden at Devonshire House under the trees ornamented with magic lanterns.

When the Marquis kissed Lady Charlotte, she did not resist him and then he found that the eagerness of her lips aroused him.

'What am I waiting for?' he had asked himself that night when he retired to bed.

The following day his grandmother had once again beseeched him to remember that there must be an heir to the Marquisate of Darincourt.

The Marquis then told himself that she was right and he was unlikely to find anyone more beautiful than Lady Charlotte.

He was certain that when she was a little older she would be an amiable and successful hostess and that was important for the parties that he intended to give both in the country and in London.

Having made up his mind, he sent a note to Lady Charlotte.

He told her that he would call on her the following Wednesday at three o'clock.

He thought that would give him time to have an early luncheon in London and then he would drive to the Earl's country house at the time he had mentioned.

He thought to save time and all the uncomfortable discussions he would buy an engagement ring and take it with him.

He chose one ring he felt particularly attractive.

It consisted of one large cabochon pearl, which the jeweller told him was one of the most perfect examples he had ever seen and it was encircled by diamonds.

The Marquis thought that he would explain to Lady Charlotte why he had decided to give her a pearl rather than a traditional diamond solitaire.

She would understand the compliment that he was paying her.

The ring was now securely in his waistcoat pocket and thinking of her made him drive a little faster.

He was planning as he travelled along, how soon the marriage would take place. And where he would take his bride for their honeymoon.

He had been abroad far too long and so it would be much more pleasant, he thought, to stay somewhere quiet and romantic in England.

Although Lady Charlotte was nineteen, the Marquis felt sure that she was innocent and pure.

She would know very little about love and it would be exciting to teach her about it.

There was one thing that he was completely assured about.

It was that he would be welcomed whole-heartedly by the Earl of Langwarde. He was well-known to be such a tremendous snob that he was laughed at behind his back.

It was therefore equally well-known why all Lady Charlotte's suitors had been sent away abruptly with a flea in their ear. They were not in the least important enough to be the Earl's son-in-law.

No one, the Marquis knew only too well, could say that about him.

He was quite certain that the Earl would insist on an extremely grand Wedding. The Prince Regent would be present and at least half the Peerage.

It was not a long way to drive to the Earl's house.

Large and very imposing it had been rebuilt in the reign of Queen Anne and it stood in a thousand acres of fine agricultural land.

The Marquis was aware that the pheasant shooting in the autumn was reported to be good. But it would not rival what he could provide at Darincourt for his friends.

The Marquis turned in at two large iron gates.

He felt as he did so that the drive itself was very picturesque and the house at the end of it was outstanding. However, it did not eclipse or even equal Darincourt.

It was recognised as one of the most famous and beautiful ancestral homes in the whole country.

He was expected, so he drew up his horses outside the front door and two grooms were waiting to take charge of his horses.

The Marquis, unlike most of his friends, preferred driving alone. He found it rather tiresome always to have a groom with him. Of course one was essential on his long journeys or if he had to stop at a Posting inn.

Now, as the two grooms ran to his horses' heads, he stepped down from the phaeton having secured his reins.

He walked up to the steps to the front door which had been already opened by a footman.

An aging butler bowed politely.

"Good afternoon, my Lord. Her Ladyship's waiting for you in the drawing room."

The Marquis handed his tall hat and driving gloves to another footman.

Then, smoothing his hair into place, he followed the butler who was going ahead.

The Marquis had visited Langwarde Hall before.

He was aware that the drawing room was unique because every piece of furniture was correct to the period of when the house had been built.

As well it was, with its soft pink curtains, a perfect background for the lovely Charlotte. It framed her fair hair and exquisitely chiselled features.

The butler then announced,

"The Marquis of Darincourt, my Lady."

The Marquis was not surprised that Charlotte was obviously waiting for him.

She turned round from the window where she was standing to hurry towards him.

She held out her hand and he kissed it gracefully before he began,

"You look very beautiful, Charlotte, and I think that you know why I have come here to see you this afternoon."

He felt that he was being slightly precipitate.

At the same time it seemed unnecessary to utter a number of unimportant words before coming to the point.

To his surprise Charlotte took her hand from his.

She turned away to walk towards the mantelpiece.

As she did so, the Marquis could see the perfection of her figure and the graceful way she moved.

He followed behind her slowly and, on reaching the fireplace, Charlotte turned round to face him.

The Marquis realised that she was behaving a little strangely and he asked her,

"What is troubling you? You don't seem as pleased to see me as I had hoped."

"I have something to tell you."

He thought that her voice seemed a little uneasy.

"What is it?" he enquired.

For a moment she was silent and then she replied,

"I am afraid it may upset you, but I have promised to marry the Duke of Nottingham."

The Marquis stared at her as if he could not believe his ears.

"The Duke of Nottingham?" he repeated.

He knew that the Duke, who had come into the title last year, was not yet twenty-one.

He had met him a few times in White's Club since he returned to London and he had thought him a rather dull and unpolished young man who would doubtless improve with age.

He had not for one moment thought that there was any competition from him where Charlotte was concerned.

He had actually, now he thought about it, seen her dance once with the Duke.

He remembered he had sat beside her at a luncheon party her father had given for her last week at his house in London.

But that Lady Charlotte should marry the Duke, or anyone except himself, left him speechless for the moment.

It was as if he had been struck by a cannonball.

"I am sorry, Clive, if this hurts you," Charlotte was saying, "and perhaps I should have stopped you coming here today, but I wanted to tell you the news myself."

The Marquis's lips tightened for a moment and then he asked,

"When did you decide to marry Nottingham rather than me?"

The question seemed to ring out between them and it was almost as if he was insisting on her answering him.

Charlotte replied faintly,

"He proposed to me – two days ago."

"And you decided, or rather your father decided for you, that it was more prestigious for you to be a Duchess than a Marchioness."

8

Now the words came from the Marquis's lips like the crack of a whip.

Charlotte turned her head away from him.

"There is no point in us discussing it," she said. "I intend to marry Derek and I am sorry if you are upset."

The Marquis thought that it would be undignified for him to say anything more.

Most certainly not what he was thinking.

He turned round sharply and walked to the door.

When he reached it and stopped, he said,

"My good wishes, Charlotte, and, of course, I hope you will be happy."

The way he spoke made it very clear that he was speaking sarcastically. There was a note of anger behind his words.

Then he walked into the hall.

He took his hat and his gloves from a footman and, running quickly down the steps, climbed into his phaeton.

He threw a guinea tip to the grooms who had held the horses for him. Then, turning them round, he started back down the drive.

He was so angry that he could not for the moment express his feelings even to himself.

It was not that emotionally he minded losing Lady Charlotte.

That he himself had been deceived, very skilfully, into thinking that she was in love with him was intolerable.

She had always spoken to him with a throb in her voice that told him she found him exciting.

She was so thrilled when he kissed her hand and he had known when he kissed her lips that she responded to him in a way he had not expected from anyone so young.

9

She had invited him a dozen times to her father's house in Park Lane and when he appeared she ran towards him with an eagerness she made no attempt to disguise.

From long experience the Marquis thought he knew every flicker of an eyelid from a woman who was in love with him.

He would have staked everything he possessed that Charlotte loved him. As much as she was ever capable of loving, knowing, as he believed, very little about it.

When it came down to brass tacks, she had pursued him even more ardently than he had pursued her.

He was sure that, if he had asked her to marry him the second or third time they met, the answer would have been 'yes.'

Now, at the very last moment, when he had made up his mind, when he had been completely certain of the answer, she had accepted the Duke of Nottingham.

'She has made a complete fool of me,' the Marquis told himself and felt his anger rising within him.

It was then, just before he reached the lodge gates, that he was aware that there was someone on the drive.

In front of him, waving her hands in the air, was a woman.

The horses had been gathering speed and so it was with difficulty that the Marquis pulled them to a standstill.

He could now see that the woman in the drive was a young girl.

As soon as the horses stopped, she ran over to the phaeton.

To the Marquis's surprise she climbed up into it.

She put down a bundle that she was carrying and said in a small frightened voice,

"Drive on!   Please – drive on!"

The Marquis looked at her and recognised who was speaking.

It was Charlotte's cousin.

He had met her or rather had had a brief glimpse of her several times at Langwarde Hall and in London.

He could not recall actually speaking to her nor had he any idea of her name.   He was just aware that she was one of the family.

She had been at one or two of the smaller and more intimate parties he had been invited to recently.

Which was when he finally realised that the Earl was pursuing him as well as his daughter.

As the girl sounded so agitated, the Marquis did as she asked and then drove his horses through the gates.

There were some cottages outside and a Church and he passed them before he asked,

"Now, what is all this about and why do you want me to take you away?"

"I must get – to London," the girl answered in a low and frightened voice, "and it's very important – that no one should see me leave."

"Are you telling me that no one in the house knows that you have left?" the Marquis enquired.

She did not answer and after a moment he went on,

"I think perhaps I should start by asking your name. I must have heard it, but you must forgive me if I have forgotten what it is."

"I am Serla Ashton," she said. "Charlotte's cousin."

"I knew that you were one of the family.   But why are you leaving the house in this strange manner?"

"I have to get away! I want to go to London!" she replied. "So please – please take me back with you."

11

"So you knew I was coming today," the Marquis said. "And you thought I would be leaving soon after I arrived and it would be a good way of securing a lift."

"That is what – I thought," Serla replied in a rather frightened voice. "And thank you, my Lord, very much for letting me travel with you."

"If you are running away without anyone knowing it, what do you intend to do when you arrive there?"

There was a pause and then Serla stammered,

"I-I am going to be – a Cyprian."

The Marquis started and then turned to look at her incredulously.

"What did you say?"

"I am going to be a – Cyprian," Serla repeated.

"Why do you say that?" the Marquis questioned.

"Gerald says that they make – a lot of money, are amusing and dance very well. And the one thing I can do is – dance."

He felt that Gerald, who was Charlotte's brother, should keep his mouth shut.

The Cyprians did a great deal more than dance.

He was aware, of course, that this girl, who seemed little more than a child, had no idea what she was saying.

"I am afraid," he said after a long pause, "that it is absolutely impossible for you to be a Cyprian."

"Why?" Serla asked.

"Because you are a lady."

He knew without looking at her that she was now wrinkling her forehead.

"So why is it impossible," she asked after she had thought for some time, "for a lady to be a Cyprian?"

"Because they live in different worlds. Your uncle would be shocked and horrified at you having such an idea, and I am sure so would your parents if they knew about it."

"My parents are dead," Serla replied.

"Then I suppose, since you are an orphan, that your uncle is looking after you," the Marquis quizzed her.

"Reluctantly, and I am sure if I disappear and never come back, he will be relieved rather than upset."

The Marquis, again surprised, turned to study her.

She was wearing a bonnet and he had not looked at her face when she had climbed into the phaeton.

He could not recall noticing her particularly when he had seen her in the past.

Now he thought she was in fact very young and had what he might call a baby face. At the same time she was very pretty.

She was quite small, much smaller than Charlotte, and she had a little round face with large eyes that seemed to dominate it.

She was certainly not beautiful in the same way as her cousin. But she was indeed exceedingly pretty.

So pretty that the Marquis felt that she typified the small child who usually appeared on the front page of a Fairytale book.

"How old are you?" he asked abruptly.

"I shall be eighteen in a month's time,"

"So you must be one of the Season's *debutantes*. Surely your uncle is having you presented at Court and arranging for you to attend the balls that all the Society *debutantes* are invited to?"

Serla laughed and it was rather a pretty sound.

"I will not be allowed to do any of those things. You don't understand. I am the black sheep of the family or rather the blot on the Family Tree they want to forget."

13

The Marquis could not help smiling at the way she described herself.

"Tell me about it," he urged her.

For the very first time since he had left Charlotte his voice was not angry or cynical.

"It is rather a long story," she replied. "And please, if I tell you why I am running away, will you promise, on your honour, not to take me back?"

"I suppose to take you back is something I really ought to do," the Marquis said.

As a matter of fact he had not thought about it. He had been so intent on his own problem.

It had not occurred to him that he should take this wayward child straight back to the house. She would most certainly get into trouble if allowed to wander about alone.

He was aware that Serla was now looking up at him anxiously.

"Do you promise on everything you hold sacred?" she asked.

The Marquis prevaricated.

"Shall I say that I promise to help you if I can, but I cannot allow you to run into danger."

"I am sure that I shall be all right when I get to London," Serla said, "and then they cannot find me."

The Marquis thought it was not only improbable but ridiculous.

However it would be kind to listen to her whole story before he made a decision.

"Start from the beginning," he suggested, "and tell me why you are blot on the Family Tree of the important Langwardes."

He could not help his voice sounding sarcastic as he spoke and Serla gave him a quick glance before she said,

"I was afraid that you would be very upset when Charlotte told you that she was going to marry the Duke."

"It was something I did not expect," he replied.

"But she is so anxious to be a Duchess and I really don't think that you would have been happy with her."

The Marquis was surprised.

"Why do you say that?" he asked.

Serla did not answer and so he suggested,

"Well, tell me first about yourself. We have plenty of time and while we are travelling at this speed no one can interrupt us."

Serla laughed.

"That is true, my Lord. Your horses are magnificent and I would love to ride one of them."

"I am sure you have been riding the Earl's horses."

"It is only occasionally that I had the chance," Serla replied, "when everyone was out or when there was not a lot for me to do, which is not often."

She gave a deep sigh and the Marquis proposed,

"Now start your story from the beginning. Why to begin with are you living at Langwarde Hall if you are not happy there?"

"I thought," Serla answered, "as you were going to marry Cousin Charlotte, that you would have heard about the family and the terrible scandal my mother caused."

"As I have been abroad for so long at the War," the Marquis said, "I missed the gossip of the *Beau Monde* and I would have been at school when the scandal happened."

Serla gave a little sigh and then began,

"Mama was the only daughter of the last Earl, who, of course, was my grandfather."

She glanced at the Marquis before she went on,

"He was like Uncle Edward in that he thought that the most important thing in life was that the Langwarde Family Tree should be filled with blue-bloods from top to bottom."

The Marquis laughed and thought that described the present Earl exactly.

"Because my Mama was his only daughter," Serla continued, "he was so determined that she should make a brilliant marriage and arranged as soon as she was eighteen that she should marry one of the Princes of Denmark."

The Marquis was listening to her and was interested enough to have for the moment forgotten his own problem.

"The Prince was rather older than Mama and she had only seen him once or twice before he finally arrived for the Wedding. My grandfather organised everything."

Serla paused for breath and continued,

"It was a huge Wedding at Langwarde with more festivities after the bride and bridegroom had gone away for the employees and tenants."

The Marquis knew that this was traditional.

"A number of distinguished guests," Serla went on, "were either to stay in the house or to come from London."

She stopped and the Marquis asked,

"What happened?"

"The night before the Wedding when everything was ready including her gown, the bridesmaids and a pile of expensive presents, Mama ran away."

"Alone, like you now?" the Marquis asked.

Serla shook her head.

"No. She ran away with Papa who was secretary to my grandfather."

Hastily, before he could say a word, Serla said,

"Papa was a gentleman, there was no doubt about that. But he did not have a title and, as you can imagine, my grandfather was so furious he almost had a stroke."

"I can well understand him being rather upset," the Marquis said. "What happened then?"

"Mama and Papa were married at the first Church they came to. When my grandfather cut Mama off without a penny and said that her name was never to be mentioned again, they found a delightful thatched cottage. It was two hundred years old and in a quiet part of the County where no one worried about the scandal they had left behind."

"But they had no money?"

"Mama fortunately had a little money that had been left her by her mother when she died. And Papa was very clever at drawing animals. He soon won such a reputation for drawing a horse or a dog that everyone in the County wanted one of his portraits."

Serla gave a little laugh as she carried on,

"I suppose we were really very poor. But Mama and Papa were so happy and the cottage was always filled with love and ever since I can remember we were always laughing."

"Then what happened?" the Marquis persisted.

"A year ago there was a terrible thunderstorm. The lightning struck our cottage and the thatch was set on fire. Papa rescued me but when he was trying to bring Mama to safety – the whole roof caved in and killed – them both."

There was a sob in Serla's voice and she had some difficulty in saying the last two words.

The Marquis drove on a little further before he said,

"So you are an orphan and I would suppose that is why you had to come and live with your uncle."

"The story of what had happened was in the local newspaper and because Mama had a title it was copied by *The Morning Post*. That was how Uncle Edward heard about it and I think too the Lord Lieutenant, who had three of Papa's pictures of his horses, wrote to him as did several other people in the County."

"So your uncle took you to live at Langwarde?"

Serla nodded.

"I suppose he meant to be kind," she said, "but, as he was ashamed of me as his father had been, I was always kept away from any of the important guests and made to help in the house rather than behave as if I was a member of the family."

"Is that why you are running away?"

"Oh no, I did not really mind doing that. There was nowhere else for me to go and I love the garden and riding in the woods if I ever have the chance."

"So what has happened to drive you away now?" the Marquis asked.

"Three days ago when Charlotte was trying to make up her mind whether she would marry you or the Duke, Uncle Edward called me into his study. He told me that Sir Hubert Kirwin wanted to marry me."

"Who is he?"

"An old man, very old, he must be well over forty and he lives ten miles away from Langwarde. He came to see Uncle Edward about some land he wanted to rent and I was introduced to him. He talked to me at luncheon."

She made a sound like a little cry.

"I never imagined for one moment that a man like that would want to marry me."

"And what did you say to your uncle?"

"I told Uncle Edward I would not marry Sir Hubert and I thought him repulsive. But he would not listen. He kept saying how lucky I was to have any man willing to make me his wife, especially one who had a title."

The Marquis felt that it was what he might have expected from such a snob.

"So you decided to run away," he suggested aloud.

"I would rather die than have a man like that touch me and I felt sure from the way he looked at me that if we were alone – he would try to kiss me."

The tone of her voice was very moving.

The Marquis knew that she had no idea that Sir Hubert would want a great deal more than just to kiss her.

"So you decided to go to London," he said after he had not spoken for nearly a minute.

"I tried to think of how I could earn enough money to live by myself. Mama had, of course, left me her money, but Uncle Edward keeps it until I was twenty-one."

"So do you really believe that you could look after yourself in London?" he asked. "With nothing in your pocket and no friends you could stay with?"

"The only thing I could think of that I could do would be to be a Cyprian and dance," Serla said.

"I have already told you it is quite impossible," the Marquis replied. "So we must think of something else."

"But what and where can I possibly go whilst we are thinking about it?" Serla enquired.

The Marquis drove on a little way further and then suddenly had an idea.

As he had been listening to Serla, he had forgotten for a moment his anger at the way Charlotte had behaved.

He well knew that his friends in White's had been aware that he was thinking of marrying her.

When he had told them that he was going to the country today, they had laughed knowingly and had wished him good luck.

When they had learnt that Charlotte had preferred a beardless young Duke to him and made a fool of him, they would not be very sympathetic. In fact many would snigger with some pleasure behind his back.

He certainly recognised that a great number of men were slightly jealous of him. Not only because of his title and his position in Society, but they envied his record in the War which had made him a hero.

He had twice received the Gold Medal for Bravery, which Wellington had given to only a few of his Officers.

The Prince Regent as well had gone out of his way to congratulate him and he had even made him the Guest of Honour at one of his parties at Carlton House.

Those who had not been honoured by such a great privilege would be only too willing to jeer now that he had been stood up by a woman.

He had always been noted for his bright ideas and for the ingenious ways that he had extricated himself from uncomfortable positions where other men would have died.

The Marquis thought now of a way that would save not only himself but also this childish girl beside him. She had no idea of what might happen to her if she wandered around London alone.

He turned the idea over mind and then said aloud,

"I have just thought of something, Serla, that would help me as well as you, if you will agree to it."

"But, of course, my Lord, I will agree to anything – you suggest," Serla replied.

Now there was almost a rapt note in her voice and the Marquis said slowly,

"It will be most humiliating for me, as I am sure you understand, when your cousin Charlotte announces her engagement to the Duke, when everyone thought that she would marry me."

"I can see it will be embarrassing for you," Serla said after a moment.

"I can most effectively turn the tables on her," the Marquis said, "if you will now allow me to anticipate her and announce immediately that you and I are engaged to be married."

Serla give a little gasp and he went on quickly,

"It will, of course, only be a pretence and neither of us will be tied to the other except for perhaps a month or two. After that you will say, as is a woman's privilege, that you feel we are not suited and we will both be free."

Serla thought for a moment and then she said,

"I understand that – you will be punishing Charlotte by announcing your engagement before she announces hers."

"That is exactly what I want to do."

"Do you think," Serla asked, "that anyone would believe that you really wanted to marry me when I am so insignificant and of no importance?"

"What I intend to do," the Marquis said, "is to take you to my grandmother. She is a very wonderful person, whom I love more than anyone else in my family. It will amuse her to see that you are very beautifully dressed and appear to the *Beau Monde* to be exactly the sort of wife that I should choose to be the Chatelaine of Darincourt."

He paused for a moment before he added,

"You will then have to act out the part exactly as Grandmama tells you and I am certain, because you are indeed very pretty, that no one will be at all surprised that I have asked you to be my wife."

Serla clasped her hands together.

"It's the most exciting thing I have ever heard!" she cried. "And I really do act fairly well. We used to have Nativity plays every year in the village, which my Mama arranged for the schoolchildren. Everyone was always very complimentary about the part I played."

"Well, here is a very big part for you to play. You have to learn it very quickly, as I intend to announce our engagement the day after tomorrow, which I hope will be before Charlotte announces hers."

"Oh, it will be," Serla said. "The Duke has gone to his Castle in Nottingham to tell his family that he is to be married. Of course they will have to know before the announcement appears in the newspapers."

"Then I think the day after tomorrow will be early enough," the Marquis said, "but it means, Serla, that you and Grandmama will have to work very rapidly."

Serla did not answer him at first and then in a small voice that he could hardly hear she said,

"Suppose I fail you and you are angry with me – "

"I am quite certain that you will not fail me," the Marquise asserted. "You will just have to be yourself and, of course, dress up for the part and no longer be afraid of being ordered to do the things no one else wants to do."

Serla gave a laugh.

"That will be wonderful, my Lord, and please don't be too upset at losing Charlotte. I don't think that she would have made you very happy."

The Marquis was surprised.

"Why should you say that?" he asked her.

"She is very difficult to live with and she is always finding fault. When she hit me this morning – "

"Hit you!" the Marquis interrupted. "What with?"

"Her hairbrush. Because she said – I had not done her hair as she wanted it done."

Serla paused before she added,

"I think actually she was rather nervous about what to say to you. But when she hits me – it always hurts."

An idea flashed through the Marquis's mind.

If a woman hit anything so small and defenceless as the girl beside him, she would doubtless hit her children when she had any.

Because he was curious, he quizzed her,

"Why else do you think that I would not have been happy with your cousin?"

"I think, as you are so important and have been so brave in the War, she would have been jealous of you."

"Jealous? Do you mean where other women might be concerned?"

"No, no! Jealous because people would admire you and you would be dominant in your own house rather than her. It is difficult to explain, but one of the reasons I was kept out of sight and made to be nothing but a servant in the house was that Charlotte was jealous of me. Although I cannot think why."

He understood exactly what she was saying.

He was beginning to think now that he had had a lucky escape.

At the same time it annoyed him as he had always considered that he could judge men and women in a more perceptive manner than most people.

He had known in the War instinctively if a soldier was lying to him and whether he was good or bad.

He had always used his instincts against the enemy and in doing so he had saved himself and his men from innumerable death-traps.

He thought that what he felt with his brain would apply in the case of women as well and therefore he would not be easily deceived.

Now if Serla was truthful, which he felt she was, he would after marrying Charlotte have found her intolerable.

Equally he felt that he would never forgive her for the way she had encouraged him and she had made him walk straight into the trap of matrimony.

He had not been aware that it was a danger, not so much to his body as to his heart and happiness.

'I will not be laughed at and made a figure of fun over a woman like that,' he told himself sharply.

They were now nearing London and he drew from his waistcoat pocket the engagement ring he had brought for Charlotte.

"I want you to put this ring on, Serla," he said, "and from this moment we are engaged to be married. No one, I repeat no one, must ever know that it is a charade. We are acting a drama which will deceive everyone who sees it."

"You make it sound very exciting," Serla enthused.

She took the ring and gave a cry of delight.

"This is absolutely beautiful. I will be very careful of it until I can give it back."

She put it on her engagement finger and looked at it with delight.

Then she said suddenly,

"Even if our engagement only lasts for a very short time, it will still be the most wonderful and exciting thing that has ever happened to me!"

CHAPTER TWO

Serla grew very quiet as they drove on into London and the Marquis knew at once that she was feeling nervous.

He was silent as well because he had been planning what he should do as soon as they arrived.

He drove through the traffic round Paddington and then turned towards Berkeley Square.

His house was the largest and most impressive in the Square. It was in fact very beautiful and its frontage extended over the whole of the South side of the Square and a garden at the back joined that of Devonshire House.

The house itself had been built for his great-great-grandfather and had been added to over the years.

The Marquis was particularly proud of his pictures. They had been much admired by the Prince Regent and he was determined that once he settled down into ordinary life he would go on collecting.

As he drew up outside his front door, two grooms came hurrying to his horses' heads.

"This is where I live, Serla. I want you to come in and I am sure that you would like a cup of tea."

"Thank you," Serla said in a low voice.

The Marquis knew what she had been thinking as they drove through the crowded streets. She would have been very frightened and lost had she come alone as she had planned.

He thought now that, whatever happened, he must look after her. She was much too pretty to be wandering about alone even in respectable Berkeley Square.

He helped her alight from the phaeton and then they walked up the red carpet and in through the front door.

He said to the butler, who was bowing to him,

"Good evening, Baxter. Is her Ladyship upstairs?"

"She's in the drawing room, my Lord."

"As I now want to see her alone, please take Miss Ashton into the morning room and bring her a cup of tea. I will have a cup myself when I come down again."

"Very good, my Lord."

The Marquis walked quickly up the staircase.

When he reached the top, he looked down to see Serla disappearing in the direction of the morning room.

Her small bundle, which contained everything that she had brought with her, was placed on a chair in the hall.

The Marquis opened the door into a very luxurious and beautiful drawing room.

His grandmother was seated near the fireplace and she was looking, although she was getting on for seventy, very lovely. She had been one of the most famous beauties of her day.

Her white hair was smartly arranged and her cheeks owed their colour to rouge and powder. Her eyelashes were slightly darkened and she was glittering with jewels.

She might have been waiting to welcome a large party of friends or to be received at Carlton House.

As the Marquis entered the room, she gave a little cry of delight and held out both her hands.

"Clive! You are back and I am waiting to hear your good news."

The Marquis walked across to her and kissed her on both cheeks.

"I am back, Grandmama, and I need your help."

"My help, dearest boy? But, of course, I am always ready to help you."

The Marquis paused for a moment before he said,

"I am announcing my engagement to Serla Ashton the day after tomorrow."

The Dowager stared at him.

"Serla Ashton?" she repeated as if she could not have heard right. "I don't understand."

The Marquis sat down beside her.

"What I am going to tell you, Grandmama, is the truth and the whole truth. But no one, I repeat no one, else must ever know it."

She held out her hand and he took it in his.

"I am going to bring off," he began slowly, "a very clever coup, but I cannot do it without you."

"You know I will do anything you ask of me," the Dowager replied, "but you told me that you were going to ask Charlotte Warde to be your wife."

"Charlotte is going to marry Nottingham!"

The Dowager looked bewildered.

"The Duke of Nottingham, but he is only a boy."

"He is just twenty-one and Charlotte has accepted him because he is a Duke."

"Oh, my dearest, I am so very sorry!" the Dowager exclaimed. "I know what you must be feeling. I felt so sure that she would make you the wife you wanted."

"But she does not want me and you know as well as I do, Grandmama, how delighted my enemies will be and how my friends will laugh at me behind my back."

27

She did not answer, but she knew that he was right. As he had been so successful in the War and, because he was of such social standing, he had enemies and many who were jealous of him.

"You said just now," the Dowager murmured, "that you are to marry Serla Ashton."

"I intend that our engagement will be announced in *The Gazette* before Charlotte has time to meet her future husband's family and have her engagement announced."

He knew as he spoke that his grandmother was far too quick-witted not to understand exactly what that meant.

People would think that they had been deliberately deceived into thinking that he was to marry Charlotte when actually he was proposing to someone else.

"Who is this woman?" she asked a little tentatively.

The Marquis then explained to her exactly what had happened after he had left Charlotte and how Serla had stopped him in the drive and climbed into his phaeton.

"She is running away," he explained, "because her uncle, who she says never liked her, is forcing her to marry Sir Hubert Kirwin."

The Dowager gave a little cry.

"Oh, not Sir Hubert! He is a most unpleasant man. I have met him once or twice and thought the way that he toadied to those more important than he was revolting."

"He has clearly toadied to the Earl who is making use of him," the Marquis said. "Apart from the fact that Serla will be a huge help to me, I asked her why she was going to London and she said that it was to be a Cyprian."

The Dowager stared at her grandson.

"A Cyprian! Does she know what that means?"

"She has not the least idea, but Charlotte's brother, Gerald, told her that they make a lot of money by dancing well."

"And who is this young woman?"

"I thought perhaps you would know more about her than I do," he replied. "She is Charlotte's cousin and her mother apparently caused a major scandal by running away the night before her Wedding to some Royal Prince."

The Dowager gave a cry.

"I know who you mean! Myrtle was lovely, one of the most beautiful *debutantes* I have ever seen."

"And you knew that she had run away?" he asked.

"Of course, I did at the time. But, when you just said 'Ashton', the name meant nothing to me."

"That was the man she ran away with."

"I remember him too," the Dowager said. "He was handsome, very polite and ran Langwarde most efficiently for the then Earl, who was the father of the present one."

"What I want you to do," the Marquis said, "is to dress Serla in the next twenty-four hours so stylishly that the gossips will never doubt that I am marrying her quite simply because she is so beautiful. They may not have the slightest idea that I am really striking at Charlotte for her disgraceful behaviour."

The Dowager Marchioness patted his hand.

"I can understand this has hurt you, dear boy," she said. "But Charlotte is not the only girl in the world and you have a wide choice."

"I am aware of that, Grandmama, but what I dislike is being made to look a fool."

"That is something no one must think you are," his grandmother said, "and I promise that if it is at all possible I will make this young girl look as lovely as her mother. Where is she by the way?"

"She is downstairs waiting to meet you. I ordered Baxter to give her a cup of tea and then I thought I would bring her up here."

"I am indeed anxious to meet her," the Dowager said. "Don't worry, my dearest boy, I understand exactly what you are trying to do and, if I cannot help you, as I wish to do, then the sooner I die the better."

"Don't talk like that, Grandmama. You know the whole family depends on you and they too have to believe that I have fallen unexpectedly but genuinely in love. And that I used Charlotte as an excuse for visiting her father's house to see Serla."

He paused for a moment before he added,

"They will surely believe that, because there must be many people who know how badly this child has been treated by the Earl. He is such an overwhelming snob that he never forgave his sister for causing a scandal and, as Serla puts it, made a blot on his precious Family Tree."

The Dowager laughed.

"It describes the Earl exactly! I always thought him a tiresome man and, of course, he must be delighted that his daughter is to become a Duchess."

"I don't know whether I am sorrier for her or for Nottingham, but everyone, Grandmama, has to believe that I have found, after a long search, the one perfect woman who I did not think existed until I met Serla."

"In other words a Fairytale come true. Of course, dearest boy, that is what we will make them believe. To me you have always looked like a Prince in a fairy story."

The Marquis laughed.

"If I was one, I could doubtless wave a magic wand and sweep all these difficulties away. As it is, I am now going downstairs to fetch Serla for your inspection."

He left the room and as he did so his grandmother looked after him with an unhappy expression in her eyes.

She had been so pleased that he had finally decided to be married, as she thought, to such a charming girl and it was essential there should be an heir to the Darincourt title.

She also thought it was a mistake for her handsome charming and rich grandson to be spending so much time with married women.

They fell into his arms far too eagerly and there was always a danger that one of their husbands might cause a scandal by demanding a duel in which inevitably someone would be hurt. Or worse still a divorce.

'How could this possibly have happened to Clive?' the Dowager Marchioness asked herself.

She realised that to be seeking his revenge like this showed that he had been deeply hurt.

She had disliked the first traces of cynicism that she had seen in his face and it was when he was being pursued by some pushy women.

It was inevitable that he should only have to raise his finger or even look in the direction of some beauty and she would then rush to his side and agree to anything he suggested. Of course if this continued he would be spoilt.

What the Dowager Marchioness minded more than anything was that he would lose all his illusions and ideals and she was well aware of them as he was growing up.

The Dowager admitted frankly that she loved her grandson more than she had loved anyone except for her husband. If she was truthful, more than her own children.

Because he had always been so kind and charming to her, she prayed fervently every night for his happiness.

It just seemed impossible that the one woman who he had decided to marry should have thrown him over, not for another man but simply for a title.

'I will not have my Clive humiliated,' the Dowager vowed to herself.

As she did so, the door of the drawing room opened and the Marquis came in leading Serla.

He had gone down the stairs to find her chatting to Baxter as she ate a large piece of iced cake.

"You'll miss the country, miss," Baxter was saying in a fatherly tone. "But his Lordship has some fine horses in the Mews, if he allows you to ride them."

"I will have to persuade him," Serla replied.

At the same time she was aware that she had no riding habit with her. When she had made up her mind to run away, there was no time to pack much. She took just what would go into a large bag she had found.

She had had no idea, when her uncle had told her to come down to his study, what he was going to tell her.

When she finally understood that he insisted on her marrying Sir Hubert Kirwin, she knew that she either had to run away or drown herself in the lake.

She had lived in a house of love and had seen how happy her father and mother had been.

She had therefore always believed that one day she would find a man who she loved and who really loved her. Then nothing else in the world would matter.

It was a revelation for her to listen to her cousin trying to make up her mind.

Should she marry the handsome Marquis, who had so distinguished himself in the War and was pursued by every woman in London? Or should she marry the Duke?

Serla personally could not understand for a moment how there could be any hesitation.

She had thought that the Duke of Nottingham was rather gauche and a tremendous bore. She had listened to him talking at the dinner table and both Charlotte and her father had hung on his words, but she thought that what he had said was not worth listening to.

In fact she could not imagine anything more ghastly than being married to a man who was so boring.

However, she was to learn that there was one man who was even worse and that was Sir Hubert Kirwin.

She had disliked him from the first moment she had seen him. He had held her hand, she thought, a little longer than was necessary.

When he had first come to luncheon, every time she looked up he was staring at her and she thought that there was an unpleasant expression in his eyes.

He had managed, although it was rather difficult, to speak to her on another occasion. They were in the garden watching the Earl play croquet with some of his guests.

Serla was expected to make herself scarce when the luncheon was finished.

She had, however, been sent to get a duster to clean some of the croquet balls and, when she returned, then Sir Hubert had more or less pounced on her.

He had paid her compliments which made her feel uncomfortable and she thought as he moved himself a little nearer to her that he was repulsive.

When later her uncle told her that she was to marry Sir Hubert, she felt as if he had struck her a blow that made her almost unconscious.

"I don't know what you mean," she had stammered. "I could – not marry Sir Hubert, he is old – and horrible."

"I have never heard such nonsense," the Earl had said angrily. "Sir Hubert is a very rich man and you are very fortunate to have any offer of marriage, especially one from a man who is so distinguished and has a title."

That was the real answer, Serla knew, and what so appealed to her uncle. To him this was a miracle in view of the disgraceful way he thought his sister had behaved.

"You will marry Sir Hubert," he said firmly, "if I have to drag you to the altar. I have fed and kept you and allowed you the privilege you do *not* deserve of living here at Langwarde."

His voice sharpened as he went on,

"Now thank goodness, I can be rid of you and as far as I am concerned the marriage will take place at once."

It was then that Serla knew that she must run away.

She knew that her uncle wished to be rid of her at once as he would be so occupied with giving his daughter the most celebrated Wedding ever at Langwarde.

Charlotte was marrying a Duke and it delighted the Earl to the point when, because of her mother's behaviour, he disliked Serla more than he ever had.

Now she realised that the Marquis's departure was a Heaven-sent opportunity.

Without thinking of anything but the menace of Sir Hubert, she flung the first things that came to hand into the bag. She left by a garden door and ran down the drive.

She had known that she had had no time to think.

She was convinced that the Marquis, having been informed by Charlotte that she was not going to marry him, would leave immediately.

She had been desperately afraid that she would be too late. In fact she had only to wait a few minutes before she saw his phaeton gliding towards her.

It was then for the first time she was afraid that he would refuse to help her as he might say that he would have nothing more to do with anyone at Langwarde Hall.

But he had been kind and even understanding.

When he had told her what he wanted her to do, she knew that, because he had helped her to escape, she would have climbed the Himalayas to please him. Or even gone down a coal mine if he had asked her to do so.

She was worried now that his grandmother, being a woman, would turn her away.

The Marquis opened the door of the drawing room.

She expected to find a very old rather disagreeable face peering at her. Instead, as she then walked forward, the Dowager exclaimed,

"You are exactly like your mother! I think I should have recognised you without being told who you are."

"You knew – Mama?" Serla asked her.

"I knew her before she ran away with your father, and we met, I think twice, after she was married and she told me that she was very very happy."

Serla looked at the Dowager with what the Marquis thought was a very touching expression in her eyes.

"You were not shocked at Mama – as everyone else was?" she asked.

"I thought that your mother was very brave and did exactly the right thing for herself, even if it did upset other people," the Dowager answered. "I can so understand her being very much in love with your good-looking father."

"Oh, thank you – thank you!" Serla cried. "No one has ever said anything – like that to me before. They have been unbelievably horrible about Mama while I have been at Langwarde and keep talking – as if she was a criminal."

"She produced you," the Dowager said, "and that must have made her even happier than ever. You are very lovely, my dear, and my grandson has told me that you are going to help him."

"As he has helped me," Serla said. "If he had not taken me away, I think I would have had to drown myself in the lake."

"That is something you must never think of doing," the Dowager cautioned. "As long as you are with me, no one will force you to marry anyone you do not love."

"I just don't know how you can be – so kind," Serla said with a small break in her voice. "And that you said such nice things about Mama makes me happy for the first time – since she died."

Now her voice broke and tears were in her eyes and the Dowager patted her hand and smiled,

"We will talk more about your mother later, but at the moment we have to concentrate on what my grandson wants. As far as I can make out, he expects me to perform a miracle in twenty-four hours."

She looked at the Marquis as she spoke.

"I have always told you, Grandmama," he replied, "that you are a miracle-worker and I want the evidence of it immediately!"

"I don't believe that Serla and I will let you down, my dear boy. You must realise, I hope, that we are going to spend a great deal of money very quickly."

Serla gave a cry of horror and the Marquis said,

"Money is no object and, of course, Grandmama, I expect you to give some very grand parties for the *Beau Monde* to meet my fiancée."

"There is nothing I shall enjoy more, dearest boy. "I am very tired of sitting here and thinking of the elegant people who crowded into this room night after night when I was married to your grandfather."

She gave a little sigh before she added,

"It was a privilege in those days to be invited to one of my parties."

"As now so it will be again," he said quickly. "You know as well as I do, Grandmama, that you only need an excuse to give one and everyone will come running."

"I just hope that you are right. Maybe I have been rather lazy lately, but now I have a good excuse for being hospitable. Mr. Simpkins will be very busy sending out the invitations."

"That is exactly what I want to hear," the Marquis said. "Now I am going to arrange with Simpkins that the announcement will appear in *The Gazette* and, of course, in *The Morning Post* and *The Times*."

"When you have finished doing that," the Dowager suggested, "Serla and I will deserve a glass of champagne."

The Marquis chuckled, bent down and then kissed his grandmother on the cheek.

"I adore you, Grandmama. You have never failed me since I was a small boy and I know you will not now."

"Be careful and don't boast," she replied. "We must play our parts very very carefully so that no one will have the least suspicion that we are not what we pretend to be."

The Marquis turned to Serla,

"I will tell Baxter that the housekeeper is to look after you and, of course, to unpack that large quantity of luggage you have brought with you."

"Now you are being unkind," Serla said. "I was so afraid that I would miss you, I just snatched up the first things I could find."

"All we have to worry about tonight," the Dowager said, "is that it is very important that Clive does not appear at his Club or anywhere else until the good news is in *The Gazette*. He will just have to make do with a quiet dinner here with only two women to amuse him!"

"How could I possibly complain," he asked, "when they are surely the two most beautiful women in London."

He walked to the door before he turned back to say,

"If I am to be staying in, don't forget to tell the chef that I would relish my favourite dishes."

He did not wait for an answer, but went out closing the door behind him

The Dowager looked at Serla.

"Now we have to work very quickly, my dear," she said, "and make you just as beautiful as your mother was when she took London by storm."

"Did she really do that?" Serla asked.

"When I look back, I remember that everyone was talking about her, saying that she was the most beautiful *debutante* there had ever been. And I would like to add that she was also the most charming. I met her when she was a girl because my husband shot with your great-uncle in the autumn, and I thought then that she was very lovely and at eighteen she was breathtaking."

"Tell me more, please tell me more," Serla begged. "It has been so horrible ever since Mama and Papa died and everyone has either said unkind things about them or looked disapproving when their names are mentioned."

"I know what you mean," the Dowager said, "but you have to forget that. You have to force yourself to look radiantly happy because you are going to marry the most handsome man in London, a man no woman, if she was in her right mind, would refuse."

"You are quite right," Serla replied in a low voice. "I cannot think how Charlotte could be so foolish."

"At the same time," the Dowager said quickly, "the one thing you must *not* do, Serla dear, is to fall in love with my grandson. You can be certain that after what he has just experienced it may well be years before we can once again persuade him to get married."

"Do you really think that because of what Charlotte has done he will hate women?" Serla asked.

The Dowager smiled.

"I don't think that he will hate women, he will just refuse to marry one. That is why you, my dear, while you go to all the parties which will be given for you, you must look around for someone you could really fall in love with as your mother fell in love with your father."

"At least I shall have the chance of meeting young men," Serla said. "When I was at Langwarde, Charlotte monopolised every man who called and if they were at all important, I was not allowed to come down to dinner."

There was no mistaking the pain in her voice.

"Now you have to shine like a star," the Dowager told her, "and as I am a good fortune-teller, I can promise you that a great number of men will try to take you away from Clive. Undoubtedly you will find one who will really make you happy."

"It all sounds far too good to be true," Serla said. "Thank you, thank you so much, I feel as if the sunshine has suddenly come out and the darkness that has covered me for so long has been swept away."

"And I promise you that it will never come back," the Dowager assured her.

*

The next day the Marquis rode early in the morning and then returned to Berkeley Square for a late breakfast.

He was not surprised to learn that Serla had already finished breakfast and was with his grandmother.

When he sent a message that he would like to see her, Serla came running down the stairs. She rushed into the study where he was wading through a pile of letters.

"You wanted me?" she asked breathlessly.

"I wanted to ask you if you had had a good night and was now ready for the fray," the Marquis smiled.

"Your grandmother has all of Bond Street arriving at any moment," Serla replied, "and I am only hoping that I shall not bankrupt you by the time we have finished!"

The Marquis laughed.

"I think that is unlikely and so you can safely leave everything to Grandmama. She is a master at organising balls, garden parties, Receptions and even Nativity Plays."

"Now she is organising me," Serla said, "and I am only frightened that I shall let her and you down and you will send me away in disgrace."

"I think that is most unlikely and if you are looking for compliments, you look very pretty the way your hair has been arranged."

"Your grandmother's lady's maid did it for me this morning, but tomorrow we are having a top hairdresser to do it before we all go to luncheon at Devonshire House."

"It is the first I have heard about it," he said.

"Actually I think that you will find your invitation with your letters and your grandmother has been asked too. She has now sent a letter to ask if she could possibly bring a young lady who is staying with her."

The Marquis smiled.

He knew that this was typical of his grandmother.

She had arranged that on the very first day of their engagement that they were having luncheon at one of the most prestigious houses in London.

He was to learn later that the Prince Regent was to be a guest and his grandmother had been aware of it.

Now, as the Marquis looked critically at Serla, he thought that she was prettier than ever and, because she was happy and excited, her eyes were shining.

Although her dress was dull and not fashionable, it did not matter at all. The translucence of her skin and the shining gold of her hair were what everyone would see.

'No one will question for a moment,' the Marquis told himself, 'that the reason I am marrying her is that I have fallen in love.'

He was to think the same when he came down to dinner to find his grandmother and Serla waiting for him. When he left the house, the *couturiers* from Bond Street were arriving with boxes and big bundles of clothes and, when he returned to the house, they were just leaving.

They seemed, he thought, somewhat exhausted, but obviously elated with the deals they had done.

Now he saw Serla dressed by his grandmother and he knew that indeed she had waved her magic wand.

Serla was wearing one of the most up to date and beautiful gowns it was possible to imagine.

Since the end of the War, decoration on the muslin gowns with high waists had become very elaborate. The one Serla was wearing was ornamented all round the hem with roses sprinkled with diamanté.

The Prince Regent had decreed that evening gowns should be décolleté and so there was quite an expanse of Serla's white skin to be seen. Round her neck she wore a single string of pearls and there were roses in her hair and on her shoes.

The Marquis thought it was impossible for anyone to look lovelier. She must have stepped out of the Fairy stories that his grandmother had read to him as a child.

"I can only say, Grandmama," he grinned, "that you are a genius. At the same time the foundation you had to work on was very receptive."

The Dowager and Serla laughed and she curtseyed to him, saying.

"Thank you kindly, sir. It is a nice compliment and we worked so hard that I would like you to say more."

The Marquis's eyes twinkled.

"Like most women you are being rather greedy and I thought you were far too shy to say anything like that."

"Now that I am feeling so beautifully dressed and so happy," Serla said, "I want to sing on the rooftops and fly up to the stars."

"I would hope you will do nothing of the sort," the Marquis replied. "But it seems rather sad that I am the sole audience of such a brilliant opening to the drama!"

"That is where you are mistaken," the Dowager answered. "We are having dinner somewhat late as I have asked quite a number of our relatives to dine with us."

The Marquis looked surprised.

"I had no idea."

"But, of course, it is the correct thing to do," the Dowager said. "If your engagement is to be announced tomorrow, the family must be told first."

"I did not think of that," the Marquis frowned, "as I suppose I should have done."

"It does not matter at all, dearest boy. I have sent grooms running in every direction and, because they are so curious, nearly everyone has accepted."

"You are much cleverer than I am, Grandmama. It never struck me for a moment that I should tell the family."

"They would certainly have complained if they had not been told," the Dowager said. "Now, as they will be arriving here at any moment, I think you should approve the seating at the table that Mr. Simpkins has left for you. And be ready to answer questions they are likely to ask."

"Good Heavens!" he then exclaimed. "What do you think they will be?"

"Where you met, which can be Langwarde and how long you have known each other."

The Marquis glanced at Serla.

"We can hardly say we met yesterday," she said, "if I am already wearing your ring."

"Shall we say a month ago?" he suggested. "I think that is actually the truth, because I saw you when I came down to Langwarde then. Of course, we can pretend that we met in London afterwards."

"The great thing is to answer as few questions as possible," the Dowager advised. "Tell them that you are thinking of the future rather than the past. And ask them what they propose giving you as a Wedding present. That will give them something else to talk about."

The Marquis laughed.

To his surprise he found that the evening was far more enjoyable than he had expected.

Because the family were so overjoyed that he was to be married they were delighted to meet Serla and were quite overcome by her appearance.

She certainly seemed to be radiantly happy and the Marquis found that she was making everyone around her laugh at the things she said.

It was indeed the spontaneous happy laughter of a child who had been given the toy she wanted.

He compared it with the rather contrived laughter that was fashionable among the women he had been with.

Serla's laughter tinkled away and it made everyone round her laugh in the same way.

When the evening ended, the family, as they said 'goodnight', were all ecstatic about the bride-to-be.

"How could you have found anyone so lovely?" the women enquired curiously.

The men patted him on the back and said,

"Very good luck, old chap. She is the prettiest thing I have ever seen and only you could have discovered her."

The Marquis was aware that just one or two of his relations remembered the scandal that had been caused by Serla's mother.

However, they did not mention it and the rest of the family were impressed that she was the niece of the Earl of Langwarde as they had hoped that Clive would take a wife whose name was the equal of his in *Debrett's Peerage.*

Luckily they were not, like the Earl, so obsessed by the Family Tree, although they were very proud of their ancestors and of the Marquis's achievements.

They drank to the health of the future bride and bridegroom at the end of dinner.

"This has certainly given us a surprise," one of the Marquis's female relatives said. "I was told only a month or so ago that you were determined to remain a bachelor, however many pretty women you met!"

"I was just waiting for the right one to come along," the Marquis answered with a smile.

Then for the first time he wondered what would happen when this charade they were acting came to an end.

'She is certain to find a husband,' he told himself.

But he could not help feeling a little uneasy. She might have to go back to the poverty he had learned she had endured.

When he retired to bed, he was thinking with some satisfaction just how much it would annoy Charlotte when she opened the newspapers and learned of his engagement.

'I have taught her a lesson she will never forget,' he said to himself. 'However angry she is, there is nothing she can do about it. Her engagement to Nottingham will come in a very poor second. I only hope everyone believes that she accepted him out of pique because I had already refused to make her my wife.'

The more he thought about it the cleverer he felt he had been.

It was only on the spur of the moment that he had decided how he would punish Charlotte and help Serla.

She was indeed very vulnerable and he recognised that when she had been so touchingly grateful for what his grandmother had said about her mother.

During the evening when she was enjoying herself, she kept glancing towards him as if to reassure herself that she was doing nothing wrong.

'She is only a child,' he thought. 'It is absolutely appalling the way she had been treated by the Earl and by Charlotte too for that matter.'

It was not surprising that she had pushed Serla into the background and humiliated her as she is so pretty.

'If nothing else,' the Marquis told himself, 'I will give her a good time while she is supposed to be engaged to me. If she falls in love with a poor man, I will make them an allowance of some sort or find him a position so that she can at least afford a few luxuries.'

He was thinking how extraordinary it had been for Serla's mother to run away the night before her Wedding and her love must have counted for her more than anything else in her life.

She had given up the whole world she belonged to, the only world she knew, and it was for a man who would never be accepted by her father.

'That is just the sort of love I want,' the Marquis mused as he turned over on his pillow.

But he knew, almost angrily, that it was something he would never find.

Charlotte had thrown him over for a higher-ranking title and it was obvious that no woman would ever think of him as an ordinary man. Inevitably he was just a wealthy Marquis with his impressive houses as a background.

'Perhaps all this fuss is just a lot of nonsense,' he tried to tell himself.

Even as he did so, he could hear Serla's melodious little voice saying that she had lived in a house of love.

'The whole thing is just an illusion worked up by the poets who write so much drivel about love.'

Even so, he knew that was what Serla sought and he had the uncomfortable feeling that for him at any rate it was out of reach.

CHAPTER THREE

The next morning the Marquis was feeling a little apprehensive.

Was the luncheon party that day with the Duchess of Devonshire, he asked himself, really a good idea?

After all it was plunging Serla straight into the deep end and she was not being given time to think. But having put everything into the hands of his grandmother, he did not like to interfere.

He was looking very smart when he came down the stairs to find the Dowager and Serla waiting for him.

"Are you ready, Grandmama?" he asked.

"We are waiting for your approval," she replied.

She indicated Serla with a wave of her hand, who was standing by the mantelpiece looking at him nervously.

The Marquis, who fancied himself as a connoisseur of women's clothes, knew that she looked perfect.

The Dowager had managed to find Serla a pale blue gown which was very pretty for a young girl. It showed off her exquisite figure and was most elegantly trimmed with frills round the hem and over the short sleeves.

On her head she had a chip straw bonnet encircled with flowers of the same blue.

"I congratulate you, Grandmama," he said. "I told you that you could perform miracles."

"If you are satisfied, that is all Serla and I ask for," the Dowager replied.

As they climbed into their carriage, Serla enthused,

"This is so exciting I feel sure that it cannot really be happening and I am just imagining it."

"You will find it very real when you get there," the Dowager said, "and don't forget to curtsey to His Royal Highness the Prince Regent."

The Marquis had been a little worried if she should be shy, especially when they were congratulated on their engagement.

The Duchess of Devonshire kissed him on both cheeks when they arrived and gushed,

"Congratulations, dearest Clive! We are so excited about your engagement and wish you every happiness."

"Thank you," the Marquis replied, "and now let me introduce my future wife."

He saw the Duchess's eyes widen as if she was a little surprised.

Then, as Serla bobbed a little curtsey and called her 'ma'am', the Marquis knew that she was behaving exactly as he wanted.

It was a luncheon party for about twenty people and the Prince Regent was the last to arrive.

As all the women swept down in a deep curtsey and the gentlemen bowed, it was a very entrancing sight. The Duchess had told the Prince Regent that this was a special occasion.

"The Marquis of Darincourt, Sire, has announced his engagement," she told him.

The Prince Regent held out his hand.

"Many congratulations," he trumpeted, "I shall look forward to your Wedding and drinking your health."

"You are very kind, Sire," the Marquis replied as he presented Serla.

When they went into luncheon, the Duke proposed their health as soon as they sat down at the table.

The Marquis was not seated by Serla but opposite her. She had two good-looking young men on either side of her and he could see her chattering away.

She was apparently not in the slightest abashed by such an important occasion and she was making the men on either side of her laugh.

Serla was very different from other women. She enjoyed everything so much that she made those she was talking to enjoy it as well. There was a ripple of laughter coming from those around her all through the luncheon.

When the long luncheon was finished, they moved into the drawing room which overlooked the garden.

The Prince Regent walked up to where the Marquis was standing with Serla.

"As you are marrying such an exceptional man," he said to her, "you will have to tell me what you want for a Wedding present."

"I know what I would like best, Sire," Serla said unexpectedly. "It would be just a very tiny peep at the magnificent treasures you have collected at Carlton House. Everyone says that they are breathtaking."

The Prince Regent was delighted. If there is one thing that pleased him it was that people should appreciate his good taste.

"You shall have your peep," he promised.

Turning to the Marquis he added,

"Do bring your beautiful fiancée here to luncheon tomorrow, Clive, and if she is interested I have some new pictures which no one has yet seen."

"She will be very honoured, Sire," he replied.

He thought with pleasure that the whole of London would be talking before midnight. Serla's success with His

Royal Highness and her invitation to luncheon would be noted in *The Court Circular*.

When they left after luncheon, the Duchess said to the Marquis,

"She is enchanting! It is so like you, Clive, to find someone unique who none of us has seen before."

She turned to the Dowager to add,

"You must, of course, all come to the ball that I am giving the week after next. If the weather is fine, the trees in the garden will all be decorated with magic lanterns and it will be very romantic for the young."

The Marquis raised her hand to his lips.

"You have always been very kind to me," he said, "and I look forward to any party you give because they are always better than anyone else's."

The Duchess laughed.

"You are flattering me, but, of course, I believe every word you say."

The Dowager said to Serla as they drove back to Berkeley Square,

"You were a great success, my dear, and I was very proud of you."

"I was so frightened," Serla replied, "of doing the wrong thing, but I enjoyed every moment of it. I have never been to such a wonderful luncheon party before."

The Marquis thought it was rather touching that she enjoyed everything so much and to please her he said,

"I hope Grandmama is providing you with a riding habit because, if we go to many of these parties where we eat and drink far too much, I think we should take some exercise in Hyde Park."

"Oh, can we really ride?" Serla sighed. "It would be marvellous."

The Marquis could see when she was excited about something that her eyes lit up like stars. There was nothing affected or pretence about her enthusiasm.

She enjoyed everything and was so thrilled about her new clothes that not only the Dowager but the women from the shops enjoyed dressing her.

"What are we doing tonight?" the Marquis asked his grandmother as they arrived back.

"We are dining with Lord and Lady Chichester and there will be dancing later. But it is quite a small party."

"That is a blessing at any rate and we shall not have to stay up too late."

Thinking that Serla looked disappointed, he added,

"If we are going to ride in Hyde Park, it means getting up early tomorrow morning."

"I am used to that," Serla said. "Sometimes when I felt very depressed I used to slip out of the house at six o'clock and ask a stable boy to saddle me a horse."

She gave a little sigh before she went on,

"When I had ridden for an hour or so, I felt I could face all the tasks that were waiting for me with everyone speaking to me as if I was something unpleasant that had crawled in – by mistake."

"Forget it!" the Marquis said sharply. "All you have to do now is enjoy yourself."

"I am enjoying every minute," Serla said in a rapt little voice. "But I know it cannot last for ever so I don't want to miss anything and sleeping is a waste of time."

"You must have your beauty sleep or you will not look as elegant as you did today," he admonished her.

"Your grandmother has been so marvellous," Serla said. "She is so nice to all the *couturiers* that they have been working all night to get my dresses ready and I have a new one to wear tonight."

"I look forward to seeing you in it," the Marquis smiled, "and now I am going to the Club."

He went off to White's and he knew that he would find his friends astounded by the notice in *The Gazette*.

At the same time they would be very curious as to who his unknown fiancée was and to learn why they had never heard of her before.

It was not as difficult as the Marquis had expected. They drank his health a dozen times and also made it quite clear that they wished to meet Serla.

"My grandmother is asking you all to a party in two or three days' time," the Marquis told them. "You will see then that I have found someone very exceptional."

"It is just like you, Darincourt," one of the older members said, "to find someone unique who all the rest of us have missed. How can you manage to be so lucky?"

"You must wait until you see Serla," the Marquis replied, "and then you can judge for yourself."

*

The party in the evening was not that small.

The Dowager had dressed Serla in a gown that was white but sprinkled all over with diamanté. As it glittered every time she moved, she looked when she was dancing in the ballroom like a small star in the firmament.

To complete the whole illusion, she had diamonds cleverly clasped into her hair. This was done, as she had told the Marquis, by the most famous hairdresser in all of the *Beau Monde* called André.

He was also, the Dowager well knew, the purveyor of a great deal of gossip and he told her the latest chatter while he was styling her hair.

The ladies in the *Beau Monde*, he related, had at first been very shocked at the Marquis's engagement to someone quite unknown.

However, when they had met with Serla and were impressed by her appearance, they understood why she had captivated him.

"I have heard, my Lady, that the future bride is to visit Carlton House tomorrow," André prattled on.

Serla had been a success at the evening party, but the next day would be, the Marquis thought, the real test.

He had seen some very sensible people, much more experienced than Serla, tremble when they had entered the Royal mansion. Others had been just completely tongue-tied when they sat down at His Royal Highness's table.

At the other extreme were women who had made an exhibition of themselves trying to attract his attention. They had laughed too loudly, talked too much and thrown themselves about in an abandoned fashion.

*

They drove to Carlton House in a closed carriage and the Marquis was hoping that Serla would be as much of a success as she had been at Devonshire House. All the same he could not be that confident.

Serla certainly looked very beautiful.

Today the Dowager had bought a pretty pink gown for Serla and it required only a few alterations. There were tiny ostrich feathers on her bonnet to match.

She looked like a rose that was just coming into bloom and because she was so excited the Marquis thought she was even prettier than she had been the previous day.

They drew up at Henry Holland's fine Corinthian Portico and the Prince's servants, in their dark blue livery trimmed with gold lace, hurried to take the Marquis's hat.

Then they went up the stairs and the Prince Regent was waiting for them and appeared delighted to see them.

He was getting rather fat, but he was graceful and his manners were always courteous and, as the Marquis knew, his charm was irresistible.

His Royal Highness had not forgotten what Serla had said to him and he insisted on her having a quick peep at some of the rooms even before luncheon.

The Chinese drawing room she had heard so much about was as fascinating as she expected. It had been an enormous extravagance of the Prince Regent, but it was so pretty that she felt it had been worth every penny.

The Marquis was in no doubt that her enthusiasm was genuine. She was thrilled with all the French furniture and an exquisite collection of *Sèvres* china.

What astonished the Marquis was that Serla seemed to know a great deal about pictures. She talked easily and without any affectation to the Prince Regent about Vernet, Greuze and Claude Lorrain.

He was simply enchanted to show her what he had recently bought and to hear her exclamations of delight.

The other guests were kept waiting while the Prince Regent showed Serla some beautiful Van Dyck pictures.

The Marquis knew that some people had laughed at him for buying them, but Serla said,

"I am sure that Your Royal Highness is being very wise in purchasing so many Dutch pictures. My father said in the years to come they would be very valuable and are in fact a very good investment."

His Royal Highness was charmed.

Serla was so entranced with the magnificent Gothic Conservatory that he had to be reminded several times that his other guests were waiting.

As they walked back to the Chinese drawing room, the Prince Regent said to the Marquis,

"She is fascinating, absolutely fascinating. She will be the perfect Chatelaine of Darincourt and will actually add not only to its beauty but also to its contents."

The Marquis thought secretly that it was something that his family would not take as a compliment.

He was astonished that Serla, looking nothing more than a child, should be able to talk so knowledgeably about furniture and pictures and he had never known a woman so interested in them before.

At luncheon, which was a large one, Serla was at the end of the table.

She seemed to be laughing and enjoying herself in a way that the Marquis knew was most acceptable. Yet it was somewhat rare at Carlton House!

When they left, Serla turned to their host,

"Thank you Sire, thank you very much. It has been like visiting Aladdin's Cave to see all the wonderful things you have collected. It is not only brilliant of Your Royal Highness, but something which I am sure is very important for our country."

"That is just what I like to think myself," the Prince Regent said in a tone of satisfaction. "You must come again, my dear, and I will show you more of the treasures I have, many of which no one else seems to appreciate."

"But they are yours, Sire," Serla replied, "and that is what is so vital. They will never be lost or forgotten."

When he said 'goodbye' to the Marquis, he put his hand on his shoulder.

"If I have my treasures, Clive, then you have yours and be careful you don't lose her. Bring her here again."

"I will indeed," the Marquis answered, "and thank you, Sire, for your boundless hospitality."

As they drove away, the Dowager said,

"Serla was undoubtedly the success of the party. Everyone present was talking about her and telling me how fortunate I was that you have found the right wife for Darincourt."

As she spoke, she glanced at her grandson and she had a little twinkle in her eyes as if teasing him. At the same time she was making very sure that he appreciated how clever she and Serla had been.

The Marquis understood and replied,

"It is all due to you, Grandmama, and I don't have to tell you that I am very grateful."

He looked across the carriage at Serla and said,

"As for you, I am quite certain that there is always a career waiting for you on the stage. I have never known anyone act a part so brilliantly."

Serla smiled.

"In fact I was not acting at all. Papa and Mama were so interested in reading about what the Prince Regent had bought, especially the French furniture."

"He sent his chef to buy it for him," the Dowager remarked, "because he was the one person in his household who spoke French."

The Marquis, still looking at Serla, asked,

"Do you really know as much about pictures as you appear to?"

"My father was a professional artist," Serla replied. "We often talked about the famous pictures he would have liked to own if he had been a rich man."

She gave a little sigh before she went on,

"It was just a dream, but whenever we went to other people's houses, my parents used to ask when we came home what I had specially noticed. That was how I learnt to recognise fine china, furniture and, of course, pictures."

"I have never heard of a better way of learning a lesson," the Dowager exclaimed. "That is what you must do with your own children when you have them."

She spoke out spontaneously and then, as there was silence, she remembered that there was little chance of her beloved grandson ever having any children.

After the way that Charlotte had behaved, he was determined not to marry anyone.

She quickly began to talk about something else and fortunately they were not far from home.

When they came into the house, the Dowager went up to her room to lie down and the Marquis to his study.

Serla pulled off her feathered bonnet and going into the drawing room, sat down at the piano.

She had never had time to play the piano when she was at Langwarde Hall. Anyway, if ever she did play a few notes, Charlotte or the Earl would inevitably find her something better to do.

She thought that, if she played very softly, no one would hear her.

She ran her fingers over the keys and began to play a piece that she had always loved and felt that the music added to the beauty of the room.

Suddenly the door opened and Baxter called out,

"Lady Charlotte Warde to see you, miss."

Serla sat up and took her hands from the keys.

Charlotte walked in looking very beautiful and with a sinking of her heart Serla knew that she was in a rage.

"I supposed that this was where I would find you," she said in a hard voice. "As you are well aware, you have absolutely no right to be here. I am taking you back with me immediately!"

Very slowly Serla rose and walked towards her.

Charlotte gazed at her elaborate gown and the mere sight of it made her explode with rage.

"How dare you!" she screeched. "How dare you run away and come to London with the Marquis!"

Serla did not answer and Charlotte went on,

"I know that he has put that absurd announcement about your engagement into *The Gazette* just to annoy me. You have no right to be here and you are coming back to Langwarde with me now."

"I cannot, Charlotte," Serla said. "I am staying here with the – Dowager Marchioness and – she wants me."

She stumbled over the last words and just prevented herself from saying that the Marquis wanted her.

"If you now expect me to believe all that stuff and nonsense," Charlotte retorted, "you are much mistaken. Stop telling lies and fetch your coat. Papa is waiting."

"I will not go back," Serla asserted. "Uncle Edward has tried to make me marry that awful man and I have run away to escape from him."

"You are very lucky that Sir Hubert or anyone else is interested in you," Charlotte snapped, "considering the shocking way your mother behaved and you are behaving as badly as she did by running away when we have all been so kind to you."

Serla did not answer.

She was wondering frantically what she should do.

She was feeling terrified. Maybe she would literally be forced by Charlotte to return to Langwarde.

Then she told herself that the Marquis needed her.

She had to stay, considering that she was supposed to be engaged to him.

"Hurry up!" Charlotte shouted. "I am not going to wait all day and I would not be surprised if Papa gives you a good whipping when we arrive home. He is appalled at your behaviour."

"I am sorry – Charlotte," Serla said in a trembling voice, "but I cannot leave – here."

"You will do as you are told," Charlotte snarled.

As she was speaking, she raised her right hand as if to strike Serla.

The door then opened and the Marquis came in.

He saw Charlotte's raised hand and Serla shrinking away from her.

"What is happening?" he asked sharply. "I am most surprised, Charlotte, to see you here."

"I have come to take Serla back home," Charlotte replied. "My father is appalled at her running away in this disgraceful fashion and you have no right, as you surely well know, to announce your engagement to her."

"I cannot see why not. I have asked Serla to marry me and she has agreed to do so."

"You cannot be serious," Charlotte replied.

There was an incredulous note in her voice.

"Of course, I am serious," the Marquis countered. "My grandmother and the rest of my family who have met Serla are delighted and they think that she is exactly the wife I should have."

"How can you say that to me?" Charlotte replied.

She was now speaking in a much lower tone than she had used before.

"If you have come from Langwarde just to take Serla back with you," the Marquis said, "I am afraid that you are wasting your time. She is staying here with my dear grandmother to chaperone her and we have already accepted many invitations from our friends. Grandmama is also giving a party to celebrate our engagement."

Charlotte lost her temper and stamped her foot.

"How dare you say such things?" she demanded. "You know quite well you wanted me to be your wife and you are piqued as I have accepted Derek Nottingham."

"It is of no interest to me whom you accept," the Marquis said loftily. "I am fortunate to find someone who is marrying me for myself and not for my title."

"I will not listen to you telling such lies," Charlotte stormed. "They are lies, lies, lies! You love me, you know you love me, and are only doing this to make me unhappy. As for this wretched girl, whom my father befriended only out of pity, he will not as her Guardian permit her to go through this farce of marrying you."

The Marquis laughed, but it had no humour in it.

"I think your father would look extremely foolish," he said, "to say the very least of it, if he tries to stop me marrying his niece because he does not think she is good enough for me."

He paused before he went on,

"And, as I should violently oppose such an action, I suggest you tell him to keep quiet and leave Serla alone."

"You will be sorry for this," Charlotte sneered.

She knew, however, that she was beaten.

She glared at the Marquis, but could find nothing more to say.

Then she turned to Serla, who was standing looking at her wide-eyed and with a very pale face.

"This is all your doing," she said in a voice that was almost a snarl. "One day I will make you sorry that you have ever been born!"

With that, holding her head high, she walked over to the door. She did not turn to look back and the Marquis did not move until the door closed behind her.

As it did so Serla gave a little sob and put her hands up to her face and then sank down into the nearest chair.

"It's all right," the Marquis said soothingly. "It's all over and there is nothing she can do to hurt you."

"But she may hurt – you," Serla murmured.

"I can look after myself," the Marquis replied, "and I am also going to look after you. You are not to be upset. We might have guessed that the notice of our engagement would make her furious."

"She will do something horrid and wicked," Serla said almost beneath her breath. "I just know it and she is cursing us as she drives away."

"Now you are merely using your imagination," the Marquis said. "It is not like you to be frightened. I am here to protect you and so, of course, is Grandmama."

"Are you – quite sure that Charlotte – will not hurt you?" Serla asked him tentatively.

The Marquis thought it very touching that she was thinking of him rather than of herself.

"She will not be able to hurt either of us," he said firmly. "She is as angry as I meant her to be and, if she talks about what has happened to anyone except her father, they will just think that she feels humiliated because I did not propose to her and preferred you. Now she is merely behaving to her own disadvantage like a woman scorned."

Serla took her hands down from her face.

"Uncle Edward cannot compel me – to go back?" she asked in a trembling voice.

"There is nothing that he can possibly do without making himself appear extremely foolish and announcing to the world that he is angry because I am to be married to his niece rather than to his daughter."

Serla drew a deep breath.

"He would not like anyone to think that," she said.

"Of course not," the Marquis agreed. "He would merely look a fool and no one can say you are not making an excellent marriage from a social point of view."

"And you will not – let me go?" Serla asked.

She sounded like a child frightened by an unhappy dream and the Marquis said a little more quietly,

"You will not leave me, Serla, until you wish to do so. I want you to enjoy what we are doing and think of it all as an amusing adventure. Something to describe in your autobiography when you are an old lady."

Serla laughed as he meant her to do.

"I shall have to wait a long time for that, but it was so wonderful today seeing Carlton House and so exciting last night and the night before. Oh, please, please don't want to be rid of me too quickly."

The Marquis smiled.

"You have a very long way to go before you find someone you want to marry and leave *me* in the lurch."

Serla wiped a tear away from the corner of her eye.

"I am so very very lucky," she said, "to have found you and everything has been really marvellous. I was so frightened that I would have to go back to Langwarde."

"Forget her! Let's just enjoy ourselves and how can Grandmama give her party if neither of us is here?"

Serla grinned.

"She is so excited about it and is making a list of the most important people one could ever imagine."

"You can be certain that they will all come. You, of course, will be the belle of the ball, otherwise not only Grandmama but I will be disappointed."

"I will try – I promise I will try," Serla assured him.

She jumped to her feet.

"I am happy again. But I do feel that Charlotte has put a curse on us and we will have to be very careful."

"I will protect you," the Marquis promised. "You can be quite certain of that."

Serla smiled at him.

"You are so kind and I think you are wonderful."

She picked up her bonnet and said,

"I will go and tell her ladyship what has happened. I am sure she will want – to know."

"Don't upset her and it also applies to you. Forget Charlotte, she is only getting her just deserts."

Serla reached the door and, as she looked back at the Marquis, she said,

"I think, if she is honest, she is very very sorry that she is not marrying you. And I can quite understand why she is feeling like that."

After she had gone, the Marquis walked across the room to the window, but he did not see the flowers in the garden or the birds singing in the trees.

He was thinking that he was starting to roll a very large cannon ball down a hill. And he did not know what would happen when it reached the bottom.

He was, however, worried that someone small like Serla might be hurt by it.

Upstairs Serla went into the Dowager's bedroom.

"I am glad you have come to see me, my dear," she said. "I was told that Charlotte Warde had called."

"She came," Serla replied, walking over to the bed, "to take me back with her."

The Dowager gave a little cry.

"She cannot do that!"

"No, the Marquis came in and told her so. She was very angry and I think that somehow she will manage – to hurt him and me."

The Dowager could see that Serla was upset, so she put out her hands towards her saying,

"Don't worry. Of course Charlotte cannot hurt you and I am certain that my grandson can look after himself."

"She is – extremely angry," Serla murmured.

"Of course she is. No woman likes to think a man who was in love with her has recovered within twenty-four hours and become engaged to someone else."

"I think really she would have liked to marry him," Serla said. "But she has been brought up by Uncle Edward to think that a great title is far better than anything else."

"Well, she has her title," the Dowager pointed out, "and now you just have to forget what has happened and for my grandson's sake go on being a success."

"He is pleased that he has hurt her," Serla said in a small voice, "but that is not right, is it?"

"I suppose if we were all perfect we would never want to hurt anyone. But being human, if someone hits us, we automatically hit back."

She sighed deeply and then said,

"What I just don't want is that this should embitter Clive and make him think that every woman is deceitful and that there is no such thing as real love."

She saw that Serla was listening and went on,

"You know that love is much more important than anything else and, because your mother was brave enough to prefer love to being a Princess, she was happy."

"So blissfully happy. If Papa was away painting a picture, when he came home Mama would run and throw her arms round him as if he had been away for a year."

"That is love," the Dowager said. "It was in the same way that I loved my husband and he loved me."

She gave another deep sigh.

"I was very lucky, Serla. I was completely happy."

"Like Papa and Mama."

"Exactly and that is what you must look for and try to find. Never, never be content with second best."

The Dowager spoke firmly and then Serla said,

"Suppose I never find anyone like that. I cannot just stay here for ever, so I shall have to find someone to look after me."

She gave a little shiver before she added,

"I can never go back now to Uncle Edward."

"Of course not, my dear, I suggest, Serla, that, as you are so sensible, you don't worry for the moment about what is going to happen in the future. Just enjoy yourself. You found it exciting today to go to Carlton House and you were a great success yesterday at Devonshire House. Just live from day to day and forget tomorrow."

"I know exactly what you are saying to me," Serla said. "You are so right, ma'am, and I am sure that it is what Mama would say as well. But I was so happy until Charlotte came and then I was afraid all over again."

She gave a little tremble as she spoke.

"You are not to be frightened," the Dowager said. "Already you are a great success and every day all the nice things people are saying about you will multiply until you will feel that you are riding on one of the stars."

Serla laughed.

"That is what I shall be doing tomorrow morning when I ride with the Marquis."

She looked at the Dowager and added,

"Now I do feel much better. I am happy again and thank you for being – so kind and understanding."

She bent and kissed the Dowager on the cheek.

"I so wish I had a grandmother like you and Clive is the luckiest man in the world because you love him."

She did not wait for her to reply, but slipped out of the room.

When she had gone, the Dowager lay back against her pillows with a worried expression on her face.

'That little child is so sweet,' she said beneath her breath, 'but very vulnerable. I am afraid while this charade is amusing for Clive she may be hurt by it. In fact I am quite sure that she will be.'

CHAPTER FOUR

The next few days were filled with activity.

There were fittings every morning, luncheon parties and dinner parties.

To Serla it was a memorable occasion when she was taken for the first time to Vauxhall Gardens.

She was thrilled with the gardens, the Rotunda, the singers and a loud brass band. The crowds varied from the smartly-dressed members of the *Beau Monde* down to the Cockney Pearly Kings and Queens.

Serla had longed to stay for the fireworks, but the Dowager had said it might be rowdy, so they went home.

Early in the morning before breakfast Serla rode with the Marquis in Rotten Row.

It was thrilling to be on a really well-bred and well-trained horse. Also to see all the other thoroughbreds and the elegance of the women riding them.

One morning after buying some bonnets in Bond Street, the Dowager drove down Rotten Row for Serla to see the fashionable ladies.

They came out at midday in open carriages holding small sunshades over their heads and the Dowager stopped the carriage for a little while so that she could talk to some of the gentlemen on horseback.

They invariably looked at Serla and waited for an introduction.

The Dowager was about to give the word to go home when a carriage came down Rotten Row that looked different from all the others.

It was painted bright green and the coachman and footman on the box were wearing white tall hats with green buttons and braiding.

Serla looked at them in surprise and at the occupant of the carriage. She was exceedingly beautiful and dressed in striking clothes and her bonnet had more ostrich feathers than any other in Rotten Row.

"Who is that?" she asked the Dowager.

"It is someone who you don't notice and should not look at."

"Why not?" Serla asked.

The Dowager hesitated and then, recalling what her grandson had told her, she replied,

"That, my dear, is a Cyprian."

Serla gave a little gasp.

"A Cyprian!" she exclaimed. "But she must be a wonderful dancer to afford such an expensive carriage and her clothes must have cost a fortune."

"She most certainly did not pay for those through her dancing," the Dowager responded.

She spoke in a way which made Serla curious and she enquired,

"Explain to me. I don't understand."

"That young woman who, as you can see is ignored by everyone like ourselves, is kept by Lord Massingham, a very rich man who can afford such luxuries."

Still Serla looked bewildered and she went on,

"He has given her a house in Chelsea and I am told has taken her abroad with him to Paris and Baden-Baden."

"But if he is prepared to be so kind to her," Serla said, "why does he not marry her?"

The Dowager gave a little laugh.

"Lord Massingham has a wife, my dear, and I think five or six children."

Serla gave an audible gasp and said in a low voice,

"I think you are saying that the lady we are talking about is his mistress."

"You are right, my dear, 'Cyprian' is a fashionable word for them, although there are a great many others."

Serla was silent.

She understood now why the Marquis had said that she could not be a Cyprian because she was a lady and she thought how silly she had been to imagine that it was the way she could earn a living.

She had read about mistresses in her history books and she had no idea that they looked like the woman who had just passed by.

This was another dangerous trap that might have happened to her if she had come to London alone.

So she was even more grateful than she had been before and she was safe because the Marquis had been kind enough to look after her.

*

The preparations for the Dowager's party were so elaborate that Serla found them bewildering.

There were to be thirty for dinner and apparently, everyone who had been invited to come in afterwards had accepted, but the large drawing room upstairs was hardly large enough to take all of them.

"You will have to take the young to the ballroom to dance almost immediately dinner is finished," the Dowager

69

said to Serla. "Otherwise there will not be room for His Royal Highness or my friends like the Duke and Duchess of Devonshire and the Duke and Duchess of Manchester."

"Is it exciting for you to give a ball here in your own house?" Serla asked in an awed tone.

The Dowager smiled.

"I have given so many balls here in the past and everyone said they were the best in the whole of London. I shall be very upset if I lose my reputation at this one."

"Of course, you will not," Serla added. "And you must look more beautiful than any of your friends."

"You forget," the Dowager replied, "that this ball is being given for you. As my grandson has already said, you will be the belle of the ball. But I will certainly try to look my best and he has already sent to Darincourt for some of the famous family jewels."

Serla gave a little jump for joy.

"I am longing to see them. One or two people have mentioned them to me and one girl said, 'I am so envious that you will wear the fantastic diamond tiara which is the finest in London, I dream that I would wear myself'."

The Dowager smiled.

"I am afraid that there are many girls who pursued Clive, not because they loved him but because they wanted to wear the Darincourt jewels and be hostess at Darincourt Hall and at this house."

"Whoever they are," Serla replied, "no one could do it as beautifully as you do, ma'am."

"Thank you, my dear, and I am only hoping that your gown will be as beautiful as I want it to be."

The Dowager had chosen a dress for Serla which no one expected.

Everyone was aware that their hostess would wear the Darincourt jewels and glitter from top to toe and so every female guest therefore would put on her largest tiara and hang ropes of diamonds or pearls round her neck.

The *debutantes* were not allowed to wear jewellery, but for this occasion they would persuade their mothers to lend them at least a necklace of small pearls and several daringly would wear a choker of small diamonds.

The Dowager kept the secret of what Serla would wear even from her grandson.

*

When the night came, he was waiting for them in the drawing room where they were to receive their guests.

Because His Royal Highness was to be present, the Marquis was wearing all his decorations. There were two diamond stars on his evening coat with a glittering cross hung just below his collar on his chest.

He was thinking that a description of the ball would appear in *The Court Circular* as well as every newspaper and Charlotte would undoubtedly be even angrier than she was already.

He wished that she could see the beautiful flowers that his grandmother had arranged in the house. The guests would enter under an arch of pink roses and lilies and all the rooms were filled with the same flowers.

When the Marquis first looked at them, he said with a smile and a twinkle in his eye,

"I know why you have chosen them, Grandmama."

"You tell me why, dear boy," she replied.

"The roses typify the older women in bloom and the lilies are the pure, untouched little *debutantes*."

"That is very perceptive of you," she replied.

The house with all the flowers and their fragrance filling the air, seemed, the Marquis thought, very romantic and this was exactly what his grandmother intended.

71

She came into the room and, although he knew her so well, he felt that she surpassed not only every woman of her age but of any age.

She was dressed in a gown of silver lamé which had a long train behind it.

There on her beautifully arranged white hair was the Darincourt tiara that was so like a Royal crown. Huge chains of diamonds encircled her neck and fell down below her waist and her wrists were covered in bracelets.

As every jewel glittered under the light from crystal chandeliers she not only looked lovely but as if she had stepped down from the stars.

The Marquis kissed her hand.

"I don't have to tell you, Grandmama," he smiled, "how beautiful you look and that every beauty in London pales beside you."

"Thank you my dearest," his grandmother replied. "You know as well as I do that I have done all this for you and I think that it will give them a great deal to talk about."

"They will be dumb with envy that words will fail them."

It was then, as the Marchioness moved towards the fireplace, which was filled with lilies, that Serla came in.

Knowing that every one of her guests would glitter and shine like a Christmas tree, the Dowager wanted Serla to look completely different.

Her gown was made of a white material that had just come from France and was as white as snow itself.

It was arranged very plainly yet, while it kept the fashion with its high waist, it seemed somehow to reveal the exquisite proportions of Serla's figure.

In contrast to the Dowager Serla wore no jewellery of any sort. Her only decoration was a little bunch of small white lilies arranged at the back of her head.

With her childlike face, golden hair and large grey eyes, she looked like an angel who had fallen down from Heaven by mistake.

The Marquis thought that it would be very difficult for any man to keep his eyes off her.

He was right, the men clustered round her like bees round a honeypot.

When they went in for dinner, Serla found herself seated between a young man who was the son of a Duke and on the other side Lord Charlton.

She had met him several times and had danced with him at her first evening at Devonshire House.

As soon as they were seated at the table, he said,

"I don't have to tell you how beautiful you look and how it is impossible to realise that there is anyone else in the room except you."

Serla smiled and whispered,

"Lower your voice or everyone will be affronted."

"Let them be," Lord Charlton said, "and promise you will give me every dance in the ballroom."

"I am sure, if I did, our hostess would be very angry with me and I should likely be sent to bed in disgrace!"

Lord Charlton laughed.

At the same time he continued to pay Serla endless compliments all through dinner.

He was very good-looking and there was something young and enthusiastic about him that she found appealing.

So many of the young men who called themselves 'bucks' were inclined to be rather sarcastic and cynical and thought that they were doing the *debutantes* a big favour if they even spoke to them.

Serla had already learnt that Lord Charlton, who had come into his father's title the previous year, was only twenty-three. He had just missed fighting in the War, but was in the Household Cavalry and like Serla adored riding.

Instead of discussing horses he kept telling her how lovely she was and was unable to speak of anything else.

The man on Serla's other side was older and clearly thought that *debutantes* were beneath his condescension.

She therefore talked for most of the dinner to Lord Charlton.

As the Dowager had told her, when the gentlemen joined the ladies, Serla led the way to the ballroom.

The best band in London was seated on a small platform and as soon as Serla appeared they started to play a dreamy waltz.

She thought it would be correct for her to open the ball with the Marquis as he was supposed to be her fiancé.

However he had been delayed in the drawing room as one of his previous loves was flirting with him in the alluring provocative manner which was accepted amongst the older and usually married women.

"I remember, Clive," she was saying to him, "that you told me you had no intention of being married."

"That is what I had intended," the Marquis replied, "but, as you can understand, I find Serla irresistible."

"And that is how I find you," the lady retorted.

She was, he thought, very lovely, but he had grown quickly bored with her simply because she had nothing to talk about unless they were making love.

'Even the most delicious dish fails if one has it at every meal,' the Marquis had thought when he left her.

It was what had happened with quite a number of his *affaires-de-coeur*.

As long as there was something mysterious as well as fascinating about a beauty, he was prepared to pursue her, but they all succumbed a little too quickly before he had really to exert himself to attract their attention.

Then as quickly he found himself growing bored. And he knew what they were going to say before they said it. He knew every artificial movement they made and every little plaintive sound of their voice.

He found himself yawning as there was nothing new, nothing to arouse his interest in them any longer.

He moved away now from the woman who had been talking to him and remembered that his grandmother had said that the young were to go to the ballroom.

'I must go and look for Serla,' the Marquis thought.

Even as he was about to do so, the Prince Regent and his party arrived.

He had not come to dinner because he had already a party to go to, but he had arranged that, as soon as dinner was finished he would bring them all to Darincourt House.

His Royal Highness was obviously in one of his better moods, laughing, talking and enjoying the crowd of men and women who were listening to him breathlessly.

The Marquis took His Royal Highness towards his grandmother.

He then paid her a dozen compliments in his usual charming style and insisted on meeting several people he had not known before and this prevented the Marquis from leaving him.

He eventually managed to go down to the ballroom.

Serla had already danced twice with Lord Charlton and one with another guest. And she was again waltzing around the room in Lord Charlton's arms.

The Marquis then drank a glass of champagne with some friends before he went back to the drawing room. He could see no reason why he should stand about waiting to dance with Serla if she was already occupied.

One of the men he had been talking to told him that she was booked until the end of the evening.

"In other words you have claimed my future bride," the Marquis said jokingly.

"Give us a fair chance," another man replied. "You have had her all day today and you will doubtless have her tomorrow. Tonight she belongs to us."

"Very well," the Marquis laughed, "you win."

He went back to the drawing room where the Prince Regent was asking for him.

The moment he appeared, another sophisticated and very alluring beauty was at his side.

"I am not allowing you to neglect me tonight, dear Clive," she pouted. "Your grandmother has told me that there is dancing for the young, but I want to talk to you."

The Marquis knew what that meant and he flirted with her good-humouredly until her place was taken by yet another of his past loves.

Serla had danced nearly a dozen dances until Lord Charlton then guided her through an open window into the garden.

She had not had time to look at it before, but she was thrilled with the beauty of the Chinese lanterns on the trees and the way the paths were lined with fairy lights.

There were seats in small discreet arbours and the young guests were making the most of them.

Lord Charlton drew her under the trees when they came to the end of the garden of Darincourt House.

Then he moved into the garden which adjoined it. The Duchess of Devonshire had told the Dowager that they were delighted for her to use their garden this evening.

Most of the guests were not aware of this, although a small gate was wide open, they had not realised that they might go through it.

Lord Charlton took Serla to where there was a seat made comfortable with cushions under a lilac tree.

"I want to talk to you," he began.

"We must not be long," Serla answered him. "As the Dowager is very busy in the drawing room, I have to be hostess in the ballroom and see that everyone is dancing."

"You need not worry about them," Lord Charlton objected. "They are all capable of looking after themselves and I really want to talk to you."

In the light from all the Chinese lanterns overhead Serla looked very lovely.

For a moment Lord Charlton could think of nothing but her beauty and then he breathed,

"I suppose you know that I am wildly and madly in love with you."

Serla gave a start.

"I did not," she said, turning her head away.

"I loved you from the first moment I saw you at Devonshire House," Lord Charlton said, "and I have lain awake thinking about you every night and wondering what the devil I can do about it."

Serla did not answer and he went on,

"Why could I not have met you before Darincourt did?"

"Because I was not in London," Serla said. "I lived in the country, but I was not very happy and all this is like a wonderful dream."

"I can understand that," Lord Charlton replied, "but what are you going to do about me?"

A memory flashed through Serla's mind.

Both the Marquis and his grandmother had said that she must eventually find herself a husband and that would be when she was no longer wanted in the charade that they were playing just to annoy Charlotte.

If she now sent Lord Charlton away, then he might never come back.

She had not thought of him as being in love with her and it was exciting to hear what he had just told her.

As she did not answer, Lord Charlton took her hand in his.

"I love you, I love you, Serla," he said. "I want you as my wife and I swear I will make you happy. Will you run away with me?"

Serla then thought of how she had already run away once and she had been so fortunate in finding the Marquis.

He had saved her from her uncle and Sir Hubert and, of course, she could not let him down.

However, one day, and it might be soon, he would have no further use for her.

Tentatively and a little nervously because she had to choose her words carefully, Serla now said,

"I am very flattered that you should want to marry me, but as you know I am engaged to Clive."

"But you don't love him," Lord Charlton asserted firmly. "I know that, you cannot deceive me. You may be impressed by him because he is a hero and is so grand. But you do *not* love him with your whole heart as I love you."

Serla knew that this was true.

She felt that because he loved her Lord Charlton was intuitively aware that she greatly admired the Marquis and was extremely grateful to him, but it was not love.

"I want you, Serla," Lord Charlton was saying. "I will give you everything in the world if it will make you happy. So please, please listen to me."

"I am listening," Serla answered. "But you know it would be just impossible for me to hurt the Marquis or do anything unkind."

"I suppose that he loves you in his own way," Lord Charlton said grudgingly. "But it is not the way that I love you and I am quite sure in my own mind that you will be happier with me than with him."

"You cannot be sure," Serla argued.

"I am sure," he replied firmly. "He has had a great many love affairs and they never lasted long. Suppose he is married to you and then does not want you anymore and you learn that he is making love to someone else. What will you do?"

"I cannot imagine it happening. Therefore I cannot tell you what I would do except to be unhappy."

"I just cannot bear to think of you unhappy!" Lord Charlton exclaimed. "I will love you totally and absolutely until we both die. Oh, Serla! Run away with me!"

As he finished speaking, he pressed his lips against her hand kissing it passionately. Then, as she could not take it away, he kissed every finger.

"I love you, I love you," he kept saying.

Serla looked at the lights in the ballroom where the music had stopped for a moment and she insisted,

"I must now go back, please don't make me get into trouble."

"You know I would never do anything to hurt you," Lord Charlton said. "Promise me, Serla, that you will think about me tonight when you go to bed and every night until we can be together."

"I have not said that we can be together."

"But think about it. I must meet you tomorrow and every day so that I can keep telling you that I love you until you tell me that you love me and not the Marquis."

Serla rose to her feet.

"What you have said – is a big surprise. I did not imagine that you would say anything like this – to me."

"There is a lot more I want to say. And you will have to tell me when I can see you alone. It will not be easy, I know that. But I must see you, I must!"

Serla did not answer, but turned to move towards the gate that they had come through.

When they reached it, Lord Charlton would not let her go past him.

"Do promise me that you will let me see you again. Anyway give me another dance as well as the next one."

"I promise you that," Serla said. "Please, I don't think you ought to tell me you love me when I am engaged to the Marquis."

"It's a free world," Lord Charlton retorted, "and no one can stop me loving you. Even if I am not saying it, you are now aware of it."

"I will think about what you have said," Serla told him in a small voice. "But please I must go back to the ballroom. I suppose that really I should not have come into the garden with you."

She vaguely remembered hearing someone say that it was very fast for a *debutante* to go into a garden alone with a man.

Lord Charlton smiled.

"It is too late now and quite frankly I don't think that anyone has noticed us."

"The Dowager will be very angry if I do anything wrong," Serla said again, "so please let's hurry back."

She began to move quickly over the grass towards the house.

"You are ridiculously lovely," Lord Charlton said. "Tonight, you look like an angel or a Goddess and I want you, I want you all to myself."

"You realise," Serla said, as they drew a little closer to the house, "I have to think about what you have said to me and please you will not tell – anyone else?"

"No, of course not. This is entirely between you and me. But however many people there are talking about you and paying you compliments, remember that I am the one who loves you."

"I shall find it difficult – to forget."

She gave him a flashing smile.

As she then stepped into the ballroom, she saw with a feeling of considerable relief that neither the Marquis nor his grandmother was there.

That meant that no one would have noticed that she had been in the garden with Lord Charlton.

She had meant to dance with someone else, but all the men seemed to be already dancing and Lord Charlton had his arm round her once again and, as they danced, he murmured,

"I love you, I love you."

He said it over and over in time to the music.

Serla could not help feeling that it was all rather fascinating.

When the dance came to an end, he wanted to take her into the garden again. Now she was wise enough to say that it was something she must not do.

Instead she danced with a rather dull young man.

He told her a long rambling story of how he had lost his money at the gambling tables and his father was angry with him.

She was relieved as Lord Charlton came to her side and insisted on dancing with her again.

She was quite certain that this was something she should not do. However, there was no one else available and he was very persistent.

The older generation had remained in the drawing room as the Prince Regent had said that he had no wish to dance and therefore none of them had left for the ballroom.

As it was essential that he should be entertained, the Dowager kept moving different ladies to his side. The Marquis realised what she was doing and helped.

He found it rather amusing to discover just how annoyed his previous lady-loves were that he had become engaged. They kept reminding him over and over again that he had always said that he would remain a bachelor.

They seemed to think it astonishing that he should eventually have been caught by such a young girl, beautiful though she was.

"I have always imagined you, dearest Clive, leading a sophisticated life," one beauty said. "I remember that you are not only sophisticated but extremely fastidious."

"I have not changed," the Marquis replied with a twinkle in his eyes.

He knew that she was furious that he should have fallen in love with someone so young.

He soon found himself carrying on the usual dual of words which he was such an expert at and every word the beauty talking to him uttered had a *double entendre.*

The Marquis had heard it all before. Although it might be amusing, there was nothing at all original in what she was saying or in his replies.

It was quite a relief when the Prince Regent, who never liked staying up very late, decided to leave.

The Marquis escorted him to the front door after he had said 'goodbye' to his grandmother.

"It has been a very great privilege to have you here, Sire," the Marquis said as he bowed.

"I have enjoyed myself. Say 'goodnight' for me to your pretty little fiancée and bring her to see me again. I was so delighted that she knew so much about my Dutch pictures. Tell her I have found another one which she has not yet seen."

"I will tell her, Sire," the Marquis replied. "And thank you for your invitation."

The Prince Regent together with the Marchioness of Cunningham, who had come with him, stepped into his carriage.

The Marquis bowed again as they drove away and then returned to the drawing room.

"Do you want me, Grandmama?" he asked her.

"I think in thirty minutes time," the Dowager said, "you can tell the band to play *God Save the King*. If we don't, the young will still be dancing at breakfast-time!"

The Marquis laughed.

"I am far too old for that."

"Not if you dance with me," a beauty piped up.

"Come and dance with me," he suggested. "And then I will end the evening as my grandmother has asked."

"It has been a really wonderful party," the beauty murmured, "and so it will be even more wonderful, Clive darling, if I can dance with you again."

"You have always been one of the best dancers I have ever known," the Marquis commented.

He recalled as he spoke that he had much enjoyed dancing with her, but otherwise she had been a bore. She was another of his *affaires-de-coeur* who he knew exactly what she would say before she said it.

However, he then took her to the ballroom and, as everyone was dancing, he drew her onto the floor.

As they went round, he saw that Serla was dancing with Lord Charlton. He thought vaguely that it was what she had been doing when he had last been in the ballroom.

She was looking happy and was obviously enjoying herself.

'She deserves it after what she had been through,' he thought, 'and I hope that Charlotte is told how lovely she looks tonight.'

"It's like old times," the beauty in his arms cooed. "Oh, Clive, I miss you so. There has never been another man I loved as I love you."

"You can scarcely expect me to believe that," the Marquis replied. "I know there are queues of young men always waiting for you to throw them a kindly glance."

The beauty laughed.

"That is what you believe."

She moved a little closer to him and whispered,

"Gerald is going North tomorrow night and I shall be alone. Is there any chance of you coming to see me just for *Auld Lang Syne*?"

"I am afraid it's quite impossible. My grandmother has plans for Serla and me and I could not upset her."

The beauty sighed.

"If I give you a key," she said after a moment, "you can let yourself in however late you are."

The Marquis did not answer.

He merely swung her round and then, as the band stopped, he told them to play *God Save the King*.

As they did so, the young guests protested.

"It's still quite early. How can you turn us away so soon when this is such a wonderful party?"

The Marquis was well aware that most of them had enjoyed it so much because the chaperones had remained upstairs and they had not been watched all the time they were dancing as at most balls.

"I am sorry," he said, "my grandmother is getting old and she must not stay up very late. But we will give another party soon."

Serla came to his side and he said in a low voice,

"We will go ahead and be ready to say 'goodbye' to the guests as they leave."

"Yes, of course," she answered.

They walked quickly back to the drawing room and did not speak until they reached it.

Only a few of the older generation were still talking to the Dowager and, when they saw the Marquis and Serla, they said 'goodbye'.

The Marquis saw them to the front door and then the younger guests collected their cloaks and hats.

"It's the best party I have ever been to," they said over and over again to the Dowager and the Marquis.

Again he promised them another party and then at last they had gone and he went back to the drawing room.

His grandmother, looking rather tired, was standing by the mantelpiece. And Serla was beside her.

"I have never known more appreciative guests," the Marquis said. "It was a marvellous party, Grandmama, and only you could have done it so well."

"I do so wish, Serla, you could have heard all the charming things everyone said about you," the Dowager said. "Including His Royal Highness, who wants you and Clive to go there to luncheon very soon as he has a new picture to show you."

"Oh, how thrilling!" Serla cried. "I would love to."

"Now Grandmama," the Marquis suggested, "you must go to bed. It's very late for you, nearly two o'clock."

"Is it really?" the Dowager asked. "Well, if I am tired it has been worth it because Serla has been such a success. Have you enjoyed the party, my dear?"

"Of course, I have," Serla answered. "And I must tell you something so exciting. I have had my first proposal of marriage."

She spoke spontaneously and then she could see the Marquis stiffen and look at her incredulously.

"What do you mean?" he demanded.

"Lord Charlton has just asked me to run away with him," Serla replied.

"I saw he was very attentive," the Dowager said, "but I had no idea that he would ask you to marry him."

"And what did you say?" the Marquis enquired.

"I said, of course, that I was engaged to you."

"I think it was great impertinence on the part of that young man to suggest such a thing," the Marquis stormed angrily, "and I have a good mind to tell him so."

Serla looked at him in surprise.

"Surely you are not angry? Your grandmother and you both said that I should try to find myself a husband and I thought when you no longer need me it might be a good idea for me to have a – friend."

She stammered over the last word and he said,

"I hardly call that a friendship. In fact it was an insult and that is how you should have treated it."

He spoke so angrily that Serla went very pale.

She clutched her hands together.

"I did not mean – to upset you," she said, "and if it happens again – I will not tell you."

With that she turned and ran from the room before the Marquis could stop her.

He actually took a few steps towards the door, but Serla had pushed it to behind her and he was too late.

It was then his grandmother said to him sharply,

"Really, Clive, I think that was very unkind of you and I have never known you to be unkind before."

"What right does Charlton have to barge in, making trouble?" the Marquis said gruffly.

"We both told Serla," the Dowager reminded him, "when you brought her to London and she became engaged to you as you wished, that when it was all over she would be able to find herself a husband amongst the young men she would meet in London."

"It is too soon," the Marquis countered angrily.

"That is no reason why she should not keep Lord Charlton, who I think is a charming young man, dangling and if she wants to marry him it would be an excellent marriage for her. He is extremely rich and has the most delightful house in Huntingdonshire."

The Marquis was silent and after a few moments, his grandmother went on,

"I suppose that you will not change your mind and would like to marry Serla yourself?"

"I have no intention of getting married," he said quickly. "Look what happened when you tried to push me into doing so with Charlotte. My friend, George Byron, was right when he wrote, '*Women are angels yet wedlock's the Devil*'."

He quoted the last words fiercely, almost as if he wanted to shout them out aloud.

"Very well, Clive, if that is your decision you are, of course, entitled to do what you want with your own life. At the same time don't be unkind to Serla. She is so sweet, the sweetest and nicest girl I have ever met in my life and I expect that she will now cry herself to sleep because you are angry with her."

He did not answer, but walked to the door.

"Goodnight, Grandmama," he called back to her, "and thank you for a magnificent party."

He went out and the Dowager stood for some time looking after him.

There was a faint smile on her lips, even though her eyes were a little worried.

Serla had gone to her room on the verge of tears.

She had thought, when she told the Marquis and his grandmother that she had received a proposal of marriage, that they would think that it was rather clever of her.

How could she have expected him to be angry?

Their engagement was only a pretence, as he had said so himself, to teach Charlotte a lesson.

'He has spoilt everything,' she whispered to herself as she undressed. 'It was a lovely party until the very end.'

She felt like crying.

But it was her fault for boasting and her mother would have thought that she was showing off.

'If Lord Charlton loves me,' she reflected, 'then I must keep it to myself, because I do realise it is the highest compliment he could pay me to want me to be his wife.'

The idea was swimming round and round in her mind and she was trying to get it into some kind of sense.

She went to the window and pulled back the curtain and the sky overhead was filled with stars.

She thought that everyone at the party seemed to be glittering in the same way.

Yet something was lacking which she had found at home in profusion with her father and mother.

She knew that it was *love*, the love they both had for each other.

It had seemed to make even the air they breathed different.

The atmosphere in their tiny cottage could never be repeated in this large and impressive house of the Marquis.

She looked up at the stars for a long time and then she prayed in a whisper,

'Please, God, give me love. The real love which Papa and Mama had and which is more precious and more wonderful than all the jewels in the world.'

She thought of all the bright diamonds flashing on the Dowager Marchioness's head. She herself did not want them, but something intangible that could only come from God.

'I want love – love,' she said again in her heart.

Then she recalled that the Marquis was angry with her and she felt again the same misery she had felt when she had left the drawing room and run up the stairs to bed.

Suddenly she heard behind her a knock on the door and she turned round wondering who it could be.

She thought perhaps that it was the Dowager, but she would not have knocked.

She moved across the room, thinking that someone must be standing outside.

Then she saw a piece of paper being pushed under the door and she bent down and picked it up.

To read it she had to carry it to the candle which was still alight by the side of her bed.

What was written was quite short and she read,

"Forgive me, I did not really mean to be angry, but what you said took me by surprise and I expect I must have been tired.

You looked much more beautiful than anyone else tonight, so think of that before you go to sleep.

Clive."

Serla read it and felt her heart give a jump for joy.

He was not angry any longer! It was her fault for telling him about Lord Charlton.

Still holding what he had written, she climbed into bed and slipped it under her pillow.

'I am happy – I am happy now,' she said to the stars that she could see through the window, 'and thank you, God, for looking after me as you always do.'

CHAPTER FIVE

There was no question of Serla riding the following morning and, when she went down to breakfast, it was to find that the Marquis had already left the house.

She went up to the Dowager's bedroom and found her still in bed with a pile of letters in front of her.

"More invitations, my dear," she said, "but we shall have to refuse them."

Serla looked surprised.

"Why?" she asked.

"Because Clive wants to go to the country to see some horses that have been delivered at Darincourt Hall and it would be a good idea if you and I both had a rest."

"I would love to see the horses," Serla smiled.

The Dowager turned over her letters.

"There are not any important balls until just before Ascot," she said, "so we can enjoy ourselves in the country without feeling that we are missing anything."

Serla was excited at the thought of the horses. It was wonderful riding before breakfast in Hyde Park with the Marquis. But it would be even better if she could gallop wildly over the fields without any interference.

She told the maid who was looking after her what to pack, but she had already had her instructions. There was nothing for her to do and a visit to Bond Street had been cancelled.

'I have so many clothes already,' Serla reflected, 'that they will need a whole room to themselves.'

She was about to go to the library when the butler came in and handed her a letter on a silver salver and when Serla took it, she guessed who it was from.

"There's also a large basket of flowers in the hall, miss, and I wonder where you'd like it to go."

Serla knew that this was also from Lord Charlton.

"I think it had better be put in my bedroom," she said. "Do you think I could take it down to the country?"

"It'll go real easily into the brake which'll carry his Lordship's valet and her Ladyship's lady's maid."

"That will be very kind," she said, "and perhaps it could be put in my bedroom at Darincourt Hall."

She thought it a mistake for the Marquis to see it, as it might make him angry with Lord Charlton again. At the same time it was so exciting to have flowers given to her for the first time in her life.

She put down the letter and said to Baxter,

"I think I will come and see the flowers before they are put with the luggage."

As she had expected, it was a large and expensive arrangement of orchids and must have cost a lot of money.

She looked at it for a while and then again asked Baxter to put it with the luggage in case it was forgotten.

She went back into the room where she had been before and picked up the note.

As she had expected, Lord Charlton told her how much he loved her and begged her to see him as soon as it was possible.

"*I cannot sleep, I cannot think, I cannot eat,*" he wrote, "*until I see you again.*

Please darling beautiful Serla, have pity on me."

Serla thought it was a cry that she could not refuse.

She therefore went to the writing table and sitting down wrote Lord Charlton a little return note.

She thanked him for the flowers and for his letter and told him that they were going to the country.

"*We shall be at Darincourt Hall,*" she wrote, "*and I will let you know when we return. Thank you again for the lovely flowers.*

Serla."

She thought that was reasonably encouraging, at the same time not accepting his passionate words of love.

'He is very young,' she thought, 'and perhaps this is the first time he has been in love. Whatever happens I must not be unkind to him or make him cynical and angry as the Marquis is because of Charlotte.'

She put the letter in an envelope and, taking it into the hall, she asked Baxter to have a footman deliver it.

She then went into the drawing room and picked up a newspaper, wondering if there could be something in *The Court Circular* about the ball last night.

The first thing she saw as she opened it was the announcement of Charlotte's engagement.

It looked quite impressive, yet she knew once again that the Marquis had won the battle.

There was a full description of the ball which the Dowager Marchioness had given and a picture of her. And there was no picture of Charlotte and Serla knew that it would please the Marquis.

She thought, however, that it was rather bad luck for Charlotte that two such important social events should be reported on the same day.

'Charlotte will hate me more than ever,' she said to herself and gave a little shiver.

The Marquis had arranged that they should leave at eleven o'clock and it was only with a tremendous effort that everything was ready by the time he wished to go.

The Dowager came down the stairs with just a few minutes to spare and she looked a little tired.

The Marquis kissed her good morning and asked,

"Are you all right, Grandmama? Is it very selfish of me to take you to the country when you could have been resting?"

"And doubtless go out to dinner this evening?" she replied. "No, my dear boy, I am happy to travel in comfort and, as soon as I reach Darincourt Hall, I will go to bed."

"That is very sensible of you and I have carried out your advice that Serla should travel with me in the phaeton while you are comfortable in the closed carriage."

It was the first that Serla had heard of this and she looked at the Marquis in some surprise.

"Are you quite sure," she said, "that I should not look after your grandmother?"

"I suspect, although she will not admit it, that she will go to sleep, while if you are with her you will chatter chatter, which will undoubtedly keep her awake."

"I don't chatter chatter," Serla retorted indignantly. "But I think what you are saying is very sensible."

Actually, she thought it would be very exciting to be travelling alone with the Marquis in the phaeton, just as she had done when she ran away. As they drove off, she found that he was thinking the same.

"The last time we were travelling like this," he said, "you were pleading with me to take you to London and you thought that you were going to earn your own living."

Because she remembered how she had said that she was going to do it, Serla blushed.

"You were so kind to me," she said quickly. "How could I have guessed that I should have a ball given for me like the marvellous one last night?"

As she spoke she thought perhaps it would remind him of Lord Charlton and he would be angry. Instead of which the Marquis replied,

"It was certainly one of Grandmama's best efforts and London will be talking of nothing else today."

The satisfaction in his voice told Serla that he had seen the newspapers and knew that Charlotte's engagement had been announced, but with less publicity than the ball.

The countryside was beautiful once they were out of the City. It was a lovely day and the sunshine spread a golden haze over everything.

Serla thought that no horses could go any faster and no man could drive in a more expert manner.

"What are you thinking about?" the Marquis asked unexpectedly.

"I was actually thinking how well you drive. Papa always said a man could either handle a horse or he could not. It was not something that you could learn."

"I think your father was right. I have loved horses ever since I can remember and I have always known that I could make them do what I wanted."

"Because you love them," she said softly. "That is what I feel when I am riding a really fine horse like yours."

"Wait until you see the new horses I am going to show you at Darincourt. I bought them a few days ago, but did not have time to tell you about them. Now they have been delivered I want to ride them as quickly as possible so that they know they belong to me."

"That will be even more thrilling than dancing or visiting Vauxhall Gardens," Serla sighed.

"Are those the two things that you are going to remember about your visit?" the Marquis asked her.

"I shall never forget how kind you are to me and how wonderful your grandmother is."

"She has enjoyed every minute of having to dress you and produce you as a dazzling star to impress the *Beau Monde*," the Marquis said. "And that reminds me, I think it will be a good idea if you call her 'Grandmama' as I do. After all that is what the world would expect you to call her if we were married."

"I would like to. I only wish I had a grandmother like her, but both of mine are dead."

The Marquis drove on and soon after one o'clock they stopped at a large Posting inn.

A private room had been engaged and, after Serla had gone upstairs and washed her face and hands, she came down to find that the Dowager had just arrived.

"Are you all right?" she asked her. "Are you quite comfortable?"

"I have to admit to having slept most of the way," she replied, "and now I am hungry and would also enjoy a glass of champagne."

"It is waiting for you," the Marquis said and put a glass into her hand and one to Serla. "Now, Grandmama, this is the first opportunity we have had to tell you what a wonderful success last night was. The newspapers are all quite right in saying that it was the most outstanding party that has taken place since the last one at Carlton House."

"Do they say that, my dear boy, I do hope they are right. Everyone seemed to enjoy themselves and everyone as they left said that Serla was the prettiest girl they had seen and you were the most fortunate man."

The Marquis smiled, but he did not respond.

When the Dowager was ready, their luncheon was served and it was all so delicious that Serla knew without asking that they had brought it with them from London.

The Marquis, however, did not wish to linger long, being anxious to arrive at Darincourt Hall.

"You children go ahead," the Dowager said as they finished their coffee. "I dislike travelling very fast and, if I am a little delayed, don't worry about me."

"I want Serla to see my horses before dark," the Marquis said as he kissed her goodbye.

They set off in the phaeton at a fast pace and Serla guessed that they would reach Darincourt at teatime.

"I suppose," she asked a little tentatively, "there is no chance of our riding this evening?"

The Marquis glanced at her and smiled.

"That is what I am thinking of doing myself."

"Oh, please, may I come with you?" Serla pleaded.

"Are you sure that you are not tired?" he asked.

"Of course, I am not tired."

"So you had a good sleep."

The way he spoke told her that he was referring to what he had said about Lord Charlton and had been upset when she went upstairs to bed.

She felt that he was waiting for an answer and after a moment she said in a low voice,

"When I read what you pushed under the door, I was happy again and I went straight to sleep."

Because it was obviously what the Marquis wanted to know, he did not reply, but drove his horses a bit faster.

Serla had heard so much about Darincourt Hall.

It was indeed all she expected it to be, only a little bigger and better. It was a very old house, having been built in the reign of Queen Elizabeth and later generations had added to it.

The red bricks had mellowed with age into a soft pink and it was so lovely that Serla felt that it was exactly the right background for the Marquis.

As they drew up outside the front door, he said,

"The brake should be here by now. It left before we did and was drawn by six horses."

"Six!" Serla exclaimed.

"I thought that you would have no riding habit and there was no other way of getting it here on time."

Serla laughed.

"It is so incredible how you always get your own way, and I think it is very clever of you."

"It is just a question of organisation," he remarked and she laughed again.

"I think the truth is that it is not the organisation but the organiser who is important."

"I will accept the compliment, but I don't want to be kept waiting."

"I will change in record time," Serla promised.

She went up the beautiful wooden staircase to what she saw was one of the State rooms, where her riding habit had been unpacked and was there waiting for her.

She thought that the Marquis's forethought was just fantastic and no one else could have thought of everything or brought it off so cleverly.

In the same way his campaign against Charlotte was so astute as no one could possibly suspect the truth.

Also waiting in her bedroom were the flowers from Lord Charlton and she just gave them a fleeting look.

At the moment she could not think of anything but that the Marquis was waiting and so were the horses.

When she ran downstairs, the butler told her that he was at the stables and a footman would show her the way.

If the house was old, the stables had certainly been brought up to date with every modern convenience.

Serla walked into the cobbled yard and she saw the Marquis inspecting six horses being walked round him and one glance told Serla that he had not exaggerated when he had said that they were outstanding.

She was sure that they all had Arab blood in them and each one looked as if it should be put into a picture by an artist such as her father had been.

The Marquis told her a little about the horses and where they came from and then he had the one he had chosen for her saddled.

As they rode out from the stable yard and into the paddock beyond it, Serla sighed,

"This is the finest horse I have ever ridden. I am sure you can say the same of yours."

"I am certainly delighted to own it. Now let's give them their heads and see how fast they can go."

They were on some flat ground which seemed to stretch out indefinitely.

As the two horses sprang into a gallop, Serla felt it was one of the most exciting things she had ever done and they rode a long way before the Marquis drew in his horse.

"That was wonderful! Wonderful!" she exclaimed.

They had not said a word to each other since they had started their ride and Serla was sure that the Marquis was thinking the same.

As they turned to go back, he quizzed her,

"Are you sorry you are missing a ball tonight?"

"I am thinking of how early I can ride tomorrow morning," Serla replied, "and not in Rotten Row but on these marvellous level fields."

"I call this area 'the gallops'. Tomorrow I will race you with two of the other horses."

"I would love that," Serla answered. "But I am so enraptured with my present mount."

She bent forward as she spoke to pat the neck of the horse and the Marquis watched her before he said,

"I was thinking last night that in the evening gown my grandmother chose for you, you outshone all the other women, but I am not certain I don't admire you even more on a horse."

"I have a feeling, if that is true," Serla replied, "that you are thinking more of the horse than of me!"

The Marquis laughed.

"That is the sort of remark I have heard you making at dinner parties, which always seems to amuse those who listen to you."

"What do you expect me to say?" Serla enquired.

"I am content with you saying the unexpected," he replied, "which makes you different from the other women, who invariably repeat and go on repeating themselves until one yawns from the sheer boredom of it!"

"That is the most frightening thing you have ever said," Serla replied. "I shall always wonder now when I am speaking whether it is something I have said before and then you are going to yawn."

The Marquis laughed again.

He reflected, as they rode on, that Serla had a very unusual way of being amusing and, unlike so many other women, she did not sulk.

He had been concerned, after what had happened last night that she would look at him reproachfully. Or to be so plaintive that he would be obliged to pity her.

Instead she had seemed so completely natural and at her ease. Perhaps after all she was not as vulnerable as his grandmother had suggested.

But there was no doubt that she had at the time been very upset.

'At least I have taken her away from Charlton,' the Marquis thought with some satisfaction. 'I will not have him interfering when things are going so well.'

When they returned to the house, they learned that the Dowager had arrived and had gone upstairs to bed.

"I will go and see her," Serla said to the Marquis, "and thank you a thousand times for the most wonderful ride I have ever had."

"I have the feeling that tomorrow morning will be even better," he replied.

She smiled at him and ran upstairs to the Dowager.

When she entered the room, it was to find that she was already in bed and she was looking, as always, very beautiful with her hair arranged and everything about her elegant and attractive.

"Oh, there you are, my child," she exclaimed as Serla came through the door. "Have you had a nice ride?"

"It was fantastic!" Serla replied.

"I am very thankful I can go to bed," the Dowager said, "and not to have to amuse anyone until tomorrow."

Serla laughed.

"You certainly did all that could be asked of you last night, ma'am. It was such a marvellous party."

Serla saw that she was very tired and kissed her.

"I am going to leave you now so that you can go to sleep. And what do you think? Clive said that I can call you 'Grandmama', as I would call you if we were married."

101

"I am very delighted for you to call me anything you like, my dear," the Dowager replied.

Serla kissed her again and said,

"Goodnight, Grandmama. No girl could have one who was so kind and understanding."

The Dowager lay back against her pillows.

'*If* they were married,' she then said to herself and emphasising the first word, 'I wonder – I just wonder.'

*

The next day was even more exciting when Serla and the Marquis rode in the morning and the afternoon.

The Dowager came down for luncheon but said that she was not having dinner with them. She was still tired and was not going to miss resting when she had the chance.

"I call that most sensible of you, Grandmama," the Marquis observed. "Since, of course, when we go back to London you will be expected to give another party in Ascot week, which will surpass the one you have already given."

"It will have to be quite different," the Dowager said, "and I must start thinking about it now."

"I just cannot believe that any party could be more perfect than the one we have already had," Serla said.

"You will be much surprised," the Marquis replied. "Grandmama's parties have always been so original. Once she produced some dancers all the way from Africa, who gave the most amazing show ever seen in Mayfair."

His grandmother laughed.

"That was a long time ago, my dear boy."

"Well, you could always repeat it," he said. "And the new generation will be as excited as the last one was."

When she was later having dinner alone with the Marquis, Serla said,

"It delights your grandmother that you want her to do so many things for you. She has told me how bored she became doing nothing and found the days very long."

"We will keep her occupied and she has always regretted having so few grandchildren. My sister has a family, but, as you know, she is in India with her husband who is the Viceroy and the children are with her."

Serla had not been aware of this, but did not say so.

"My other sister," the Marquis went on, "is married to a Scandinavian Prince and they visit England only very occasionally."

"So you are the only one here?"

"That is exactly why she makes such a fuss of me," the Marquis replied. "I try to please her, but I cannot do everything she wants."

The way he spoke told Serla without further words that he had no intention of getting married.

Yet it was the one thing his grandmother really wanted for him, so tactfully she changed the conversation.

But she thought she would be wise to keep up her 'friendship' if that was the right word, with Lord Charlton.

*

The next evening the Marquis said in an irritated voice,

"I shall have to go to London tomorrow morning."

"Oh, but why?" Serla asked him, thinking that she would not be able to ride.

"I have had a message that His Royal Highness particularly wants to see me. It was explained to him that I had gone to the country, but he still insists that I should go to Carlton House and so I cannot possibly refuse."

"Will you be away long?" Serla enquired.

"I will be back, if at all possible, before dinner, but I find it extremely annoying."

He thought for a moment and then added,

"I just cannot think why His Royal Highness cannot wait for my return. It's a terrible bore to have to return just as I have arrived here."

Serla knew that he was thinking of the horses and there were still two that he had not ridden. He was very determined to try them all and decide which was the best.

"Come back just as quickly as you can," Serla said. "Perhaps if you are lucky it will be before it is dark."

"I know what you are thinking, but I am afraid we shall have to accept it as a wasted day and there is nothing we can do about it."

"I shall not waste it as I want to explore the house and you did promise me that you would show me the secret passages from the time when Queen Mary was persecuting the Protestants."

"You shall see them on my return," he promised. "They are, I am told, the best examples in the country."

"Then hurry back! Hurry! Hurry!" Serla repeated and he laughed.

*

The next day she did explore a great deal of the house before the Dowager came down to luncheon.

Serla was extremely impressed with the library and it contained, so the Curator told her, five thousand books.

She was delighted with the music room and would have sat there playing the piano if she had not wanted to see the Picture Gallery. It was, the Dowager told her, an exceptional collection to be owned by any one family.

"Are you not frightened that they might be stolen?" Serla asked.

"Clive has thought of that and I believed that they were not very well protected by my husband. But he has had the grooms taught to shoot as well as the footmen."

She paused before she added,

"If that is known locally, which of course it is, any burglar will be afraid to risk it even for a fine painting."

"The Marquis thinks of everything," Serla said.

She found that the garden was almost as interesting as the house.

There was an ancient sun dial in the Rose Garden, which was very lovely and there was a huge fountain on the green lawn behind the house, which she was told had been put there in Queen Elizabeth's time. And there was a Herb Garden, which had been created in the reign of King Charles II.

There was so much to see and so much to admire, that the day passed very quickly even though she was alone most of the time.

It was getting dusk and the sun was now beginning to sink a little.

It was still not far off dinnertime when she realised that there was still no sign of the Marquis.

"I do hope," she said to the Dowager, " that Clive will not be kept in London for another day. I am so looking forward to riding with him tomorrow morning."

"He will return here if it is humanly possible, but you know exactly what Royalty are like. When they want something, they will never think of other people's feelings, only their own requirements."

However there was still no sign of him when dinner was ready and Serla ate it alone because the Dowager had retired to bed.

The food was really delicious and the butler, who had been in the family for forty years, talked to her while he served the dishes.

He told her just how proud everyone was that the Marquis had been so brave in the War and the anxiety that the family had been through in case he was killed. And there would then be no direct heir to carry on the title.

"That's why, miss, we're all ever so delighted that you're going to marry his Lordship," the butler added.

Serla felt it was wrong that she should be deceiving these people, who believed in a way that they too were part of the family.

There was nothing that she could say except that she hoped the Marquis would be happy.

By the time she left the dining room it was getting dark. In fact the last rays of the sun were sinking behind the great oak trees in the Park.

As Serla went into the hall, she glanced through the open front door.

She was hoping that she would see the Marquis's phaeton coming up the drive, but there was no sign of him.

She went into one of the beautiful sitting rooms where the windows looked out over the garden.

She had just picked up a book when one of the footmen came in to say,

"There be a woman at the front door, miss, who's askin' if you'll help her."

"A woman!" Serla exclaimed. "Who is she?"

She felt that it must be someone from the village and yet she could not imagine why they should have asked for her rather than the Dowager.

But, of course, she could think that, as she was to marry the Marquis, she was one of the family.

She rose from the sofa where she was sitting and put down her book.

"I will come and speak to her."

There was only one footman on duty in the hall as now her dinner was finished the others were having theirs.

The woman was outside the front door, a little way from it, as if she was too shy to come closer.

Serla stepped out towards her.

"Can I help you?" she asked.

"It's me dog, miss," the woman said. "'E's bin 'urt and I think lovin' animals you'd do somethin' for 'im."

"Yes, of course," Serla agreed. "Where is he?"

"'E be down there by that tree," the woman replied, pointing to one of the oaks that lined the driveway.

"I will come and see what I can do."

Serla felt that she should take something with her, but, if the dog was not large, she could either carry it back to the house or take it to the stables.

She walked to the courtyard and down the drive.

As she did so, she glanced at the woman beside her and realised that she was a Romany gypsy. There was no mistaking the darkness of her skin and the black Romany hair showed beneath the coloured kerchief on her head.

Slowly, as she did not want to seem rude, she said,

"I think perhaps you are a Romany."

"That's right, miss," the gypsy replied. "We be just passin' through, but I thinks you'd be kinder to my dog than the villagers who're often afraid of us gypsies."

Serla knew this to be true.

Although her father and mother had often talked to the gypsies and so had she, the local villagers would have nothing to do with them, except occasionally when the girls wanted their fortune told.

When the gypsies appeared, as they did at the hop-picking time, the villagers ostentatiously used to lock away their cocks and hens. If anything was missing in the time the gypsies were in the vicinity, they were always accused of stealing.

Serla reached the first oak tree in the Park which was where she expected to find the dog.

However the gypsy woman moved on.

"It be a little further," she said, "by yon tree there."

She pointed ahead to where there was a very large oak and, as it was now dusk, it was difficult to see clearly beneath it because of the thickness of the branches.

They reached the oak and Serla looked down on the ground expecting to see the dog lying on the far side of it.

Then, as she did so, a heavy cloth was thrown over her head.

She tried to scream and struggled as a man picked her up in his arms.

There was nothing she could do and the weight of the cloth over her head made it impossible to even breathe.

She felt someone tying a rope round her ankles.

Then the man who was carrying her, and he seemed very strong, began to walk away.

Serla knew despairingly that she was out of sight of the house.

It just seemed incredible and impossible that it was happening, yet it was.

The man's arms tightened and he then went faster.

'Help me,' she cried silently. 'Oh, please God help me!'

*

The Marquis had pushed his horses as hard as he could, but knew, as he turned in at the gates of Darincourt

Hall, that it was far too late for him to see his new horses and Serla might even have gone to bed.

He had begun to believe that he would never get away from London and might even have to stay the night.

He had to admit, however, that the Prince Regent had been right in sending for him. It all concerned some trouble with the French over an incident that had occurred when the Army of Occupation was stationed in Cambrai.

At the time when it happened the Marquis had been there and he could explain exactly what had transpired.

The War Office had not been able to get in touch with the Duke of Wellington, who was in Scotland.

To the Prince Regent's delight he was consulted.

He had been kept out of many things that concerned the governing of the country and he was therefore always thrilled when his advice was asked and he had the answer.

He had realised at once that the one person who in Wellington's absence could be of use was the Marquis and that was his reason for insisting on his return to London.

The Marquis had been able to tell the War Office what they wanted to know. Yet needless to say it had taken a very long time and he had been asked a great number of questions, which he had thought unnecessary.

As soon as he was free, he jumped into his phaeton and set off at once for Darincourt.

It took a long time, although he did not stop to eat or drink, and it was dark when he finally arrived.

The stars, however, were coming out and there was a full moon and that was no compensation for knowing that it was too late to go to the stables.

He left his phaeton and walked up to the front door.

It was already opened by Desbury, the old butler.

"I thinks you'd forgotten all about us, my Lord," he said when the Marquis appeared.

"I came as soon as I could. I suppose everyone is in bed."

"Her Ladyship is, my Lord, but I'm a bit worried as Miss Ashton has not returned."

"Not returned? What do you mean by that?"

Desbury looked towards one of the footmen.

"A woman called to see her, my Lord, about two hours ago. She said her dog was injured, but Miss Ashton has not come back."

"A woman, what woman?" the Marquis asked.

The footman came forward as Desbury beckoned.

"'Twas a young woman, my Lord, but no one as comes from the village or I'd have known her."

"What was she like?" the Marquis asked.

The footman scratched his head before he replied,

"Well, my Lord, I may not be right, but I thinks her be a gypsy."

"A gypsy and Miss Ashton has not returned?"

"No, my Lord."

"You are quite certain of that?"

"As it happens, my Lord," Desbury said, "I have been up to Miss Ashton's bedroom just in case she'd come in and no one had noticed her, but the maid who's been looking after her said there's been no sign of her."

The Marquis's instinct told him at once that there was something very wrong.

It was the same instinct which had warned him in the War when things were becoming dangerous.

Without saying anything more, he ran down the steps and walked very quickly towards the stables.

The Head Groom was there as he had been waiting for the phaeton to come back.

The Marquis gave his orders sharply and clearly. It was the way he had given orders before going into battle.

After the first glance when he began speaking, the grooms listened attentively, ran to obey and five minutes later four of them were mounted on horses.

The Marquis swung himself onto the saddle of the one he had chosen to ride.

The Head Groom then handed him a pistol that was always kept in the phaeton for fear of highwaymen.

The Marquis put it in his pocket and he had already told the four grooms that they were to be armed.

Then, as they waited, he said,

"Now you quite understand. You each ride in the direction I have told you to go. At the first sign of a gypsy caravan you make an owl-hoot several times. As it is a clear calm evening, I shall undoubtedly hear it. All the rest of you will be waiting for the signal and when it comes you ride straight in that direction."

He paused to see if they were all listening to him.

"Whoever sees the gypsies," he went on, "is not to go near to them. Just continue every four or five minutes repeating an owl-hoot. As you are all countrymen, you can hoot so that the gypsies don't realise what we are doing. Do you understand?"

"Yes, my Lord, we understand," they murmured.

"Then, when you join me, I will give you the next orders," the Marquis said. "Go now quickly."

The men obeyed him and then he slowly rode down the drive in the direction that the footman told him Serla had gone.

It seemed incredible that this should happen to her.

At the same time he was almost certain that she had been abducted on Charlotte's orders.

If she was carried far it would be impossible to find her and the only hope was to track her down immediately.

He knew that gypsies would not travel far at night and, if they camped and one of his men discovered her, then he would know exactly what to do.

It was, he feared, only a chance that he had got it right, yet every instinct now told him that this was what was needed if he was to save Serla.

'It is my fault,' he chided himself. 'I should have anticipated that Charlotte would not let her get away with it so easily. As I thought before, *Hell hath no fury like a woman scorned.*'

CHAPTER SIX

Serla felt herself thrown down roughly onto what seemed to be a hard bed.

Then, as wheels began turning underneath her, she knew that she was in a caravan.

It was being driven at a very much faster speed than gypsies usually achieved and, as the road was so rough, she felt herself being bumped from side to side.

She tried to think what could be happening or who was responsible for treating her in such a way.

Then, almost as if a voice was telling her, she knew that it was Charlotte. Of course it was Charlotte, avenging herself because the Marquis had turned the tables on her.

It was difficult to breathe and as difficult to think.

Serla hoped she would not faint from suffocation as the thick cloth over her face made her feel as if she was gasping for breath.

Without her even being aware of it, while he was carrying her, the gypsy had tied a rope round her waist.

When he had thrown her down on the bed, he had tightened the rope so that she could not move her arms and her ankles had already been tied before he started to take her away from the Park.

It was difficult to think or to formulate anything in her mind, until unexpectedly the heavy rug was then taken off her face.

The caravan was still moving at a steady speed and there were no lights inside it.

Serla became aware that it was a woman who was beside her and who had made it easier for her to breathe.

She drew in a deep breath and felt, either from lack of air or fear, that her lips were dry.

"Where am – I?" she asked unsteadily.

The gypsy woman did not reply, she merely put her finger on Serla's lips to ensure silence.

There was nothing Serla could do but lie still in the darkness, terrified as to what would happen to her at the end of the journey.

Perhaps Charlotte had told the gypsies to dispose of her in some way. She could be drowned in a stream that they were passing.

It was then she began to pray again for help, not only to God but to the Marquis as well.

He had not yet come back when she left the house and perhaps when he did he would not enquire where she was, but would take it that she had gone up to bed.

Every possibility she thought of seemed to be more frightening than the last and she could only send a cry of help towards him.

'Help me, help me, I am being taken away from you and you may never see me again. Help! *Help me*!'

It was a cry that came from the depths of her heart.

Serla knew that there was no one else who could save her, no one else would have any idea of the danger she was in.

'As we made plans together, talked together and thought together,' she told herself, 'I am sure that I can make him hear me.'

She remembered how her father had told her that in India the people often communicated with each other by sheer thought. A man who was hundreds of miles away from his family would know when one of them had died and he could be called to their side if they were in trouble.

'If the Indians can do it, I can too,' she told herself.

She went on calling out to the Marquis in her heart and begged him to hear her with every nerve in her body.

'Help me! Help me! Oh, God, make him hear me.'

The caravan must have travelled for nearly an hour and then it seemed to turn off as if leaving the road. It was bumping over what Serla thought must be thick grass.

'If we are going to camp for the night,' she told herself, 'there is a chance of Clive finding me.'

He would be home by now and surely he would ask where she was.

She tried to remember at what time the footmen changed their duties and when the night-footman came on duty. And he would not know what had happened.

The only thing she could do was to go on praying for the Marquis to hear her.

Outside she could hear other caravans near to the one she was in and then, when the sound of their wheels ceased, there were voices talking to each other.

They seemed to be busy about something and Serla wondered what it was.

Then she was aware that there was a light coming in through the sides of the door in the front of her caravan.

She guessed that a fire had been kindled and she was sure of this when later there was a smell of food.

She thought that it must be rabbit as they would have snared them in the woods while they were camping during the day.

She wondered if she would be offered anything to eat, perhaps as a prisoner they would give her nothing.

If they were in a great hurry to go further away from Darincourt Hall, she would probably not be given any food until tomorrow.

It was only supposition, just ideas moving through her mind.

What she longed to do was to scream for help, but she knew that it would do no good. If she made a noise they might throw the heavy rug over her again so that she could not breathe.

Once again she was praying.

'Help me, Almighty God, please help me. Send the Marquis to me. He is the only one who can rescue me.'

She wanted him so desperately she felt just as if she could see him looking handsome and so sure of himself. So very much the hero he had been in the War.

It was then, as she called again for him in her mind, that she knew that she loved him.

It was hopeless, a love that could never be requited and there was nothing she could do about it.

As she cried out to him for help, she knew that her heart and soul called for him too.

What she was feeling was love.

The love that she had always wanted and the love that she believed was perfect and came from God.

But only if the man she loved could return the love she was offering him with all her heart.

*

Waiting for the cries of the owl, the Marquis was calculating.

Just how long was it now since, according to the footman, Serla had gone away with the gypsy woman. It must be, he thought, nearly two hours.

Now the night had closed in and there was a moon high over the trees and the sky was filled with stars.

He thought, as he waited, that each minute seemed to take an hour.

Above all was the fear that he would not trace the gypsies and Serla would be carried too far from Darincourt for him ever to catch up with her.

'Gypsies cannot travel very fast,' he told himself as their rumbling caravans could only move slowly and they would doubtless have spare horses that were usually led.

'Where can she be?' he kept asking himself.

At the same time he listened intently, feeling that he must soon hear the sound that he was waiting for.

Then, as he was feeling desperate, he heard it.

It was undoubtedly the sound of an owl far in the distance and to the South.

He had expected the gypsies to go in the direction of London, but they were moving South.

He then sent up his own hoot, hoping that the other grooms who had ridden in other directions would hear it.

He made the cry twice more before he rode towards the hoot he had heard.

As he galloped over the fields, he heard it nearer each time the groom made it.

Then unexpectedly by a small copse he heard it so loudly that it made him start.

He pushed his horse forward and a moment later was with the groom he was seeking.

"You have found her, Henry?" he asked keeping his voice very low.

"Them gypsies be just across the road, my Lord, and campin' in the field beyond it."

"Good boy!" the Marquis exclaimed.

As he spoke he glanced back over the field.

He saw in the moonlight two of the other grooms approaching him at a gallop. They were still some distance away and he said to Henry in a whisper,

"How many caravans are there?"

"I thinks five, my Lord."

The Marquis reckoned that there would be five men at least and perhaps some boys.

But with four of his men fully armed, there should be no trouble if they took them by surprise.

He waited until the other grooms came up to him and fortunately they were to see him in the moonlight.

The Marquis wasted no time in talking.

"Follow me and have your pistols at the ready."

He had seen that there was a gate out of the field they were in now leading onto the road.

A bit further up was where the gypsies had camped.

When the Marquis reached them, he saw that Henry had been right in telling him that there were five caravans and they seemed hardly enough for the number of gypsies clustered round the fire.

They were all eating out of bowls what had been cooked on the fire.

There was no gate to the field and, as the Marquis rode in, the gypsies looked up in surprise.

Then three of the men sprang to their feet, followed by the others.

The Marquis drew up beside them with the three grooms just behind him.

"I want to speak to your Leader or Chief," he said.

An older dark-skinned man with lanky black hair hanging down on either side of his face, was, the Marquis thought, a Romany.

"That be me," he said.

"I wish to speak to you."

Somewhat reluctantly, he thought, the gypsy moved a little nearer to him.

The Marquis, lowering his voice, asserted,

"You have a young lady you have taken from my house not far away. What were you paid to abduct her?"

The gypsy started and then said quickly,

"No sir, no lady, only gypsies 'ere."

"That is not true!" the Marquis said. "Tell me what you were paid to take her away and I will double it if you give her back to me."

He paused and then, as he felt that the gypsy was about to refuse, he added,

"Otherwise we will take her by force. I have three men with me and others on their way."

As he spoke, he drew out his pistol.

As if it was an unspoken command, all three of the grooms brought theirs out from their pockets and then held them pointing in the direction of the gypsy.

The Gypsy Chief eyed them and in a very surly voice replied,

"Ten pounds, I were given, ten pounds!"

The Marquis put his hand into his inside pocket and drew out his wallet.

He took from it a bank note of that denomination and bending down handed it to the gypsy.

"Now bring me the lady," he demanded sharply.

The Gypsy Chief took the note and thrust it into his clothes.

Then he snapped his fingers and spoke in Romany to two of the women.

They climbed up into one of the caravans.

While the Marquis waited, the other gypsies stared at him without moving.

He knew that they were scared and they made no attempt to move as if they knew that unarmed they had no chance of winning a battle.

It now seemed to the Marquis that the women were taking a very long time.

And he was not to know that they were undoing the ropes round Serla's body.

She had, however, heard the Marquis's voice.

Although she wanted to scream and tell him where she was, she knew because he was speaking quietly that it would be a mistake.

It was almost as if he was telling her to keep silent and not to make a scene unless it was absolutely necessary.

The two women pulled off the rope round her body and undid the one round her ankles.

Then they pulled Serla, who was still lying on the bed, towards the door of the caravan.

Because the ropes had hurt her, it was difficult for the moment to try to walk.

As the women opened the caravan door, she heard the Marquis give a sharp order.

The man who was the Chief and who Serla knew had carried her when she was in the Park held out his arms.

One glance told Serla that the Marquis was still on his horse.

She understood why the man was lifting her from the caravan not onto the ground, but into his arms and then he carried her the short distance to the Marquis.

He lifted her up and the Marquis put his arm round Serla and seated her on the saddle in front of him.

Then, as he tightened his arm round her, she clung to him, hiding her face against his shoulder.

The Marquis turned to the Gypsy Chief and said,

"Another time be more careful and don't try again to abduct a lady. If you do, you might then find yourself fighting the men I have here and it is doubtful if any of you would survive."

The Gypsy Chief did not answer.

The Marquis hoped that he had frightened him.

Then he turned his horse round and moved away from the camp and back onto the road.

Now, as the grooms joined him, the Marquis said,

"You have done well and exactly what I told you. Now you can ride home and try to find Ben on the way. Call him with the owl-hoot as perhaps he did not hear it."

"Very good, my Lord," they chorused.

Then they all rode off ahead, excited and delighted by their success in rescuing the lost lady.

The Marquis rode on for a little while and then he realised that Serla was in tears.

"It's all right," he said. "It's all over, but it must have been very frightening."

"I thought you would never hear me," Serla sobbed, "but I was calling for you – calling for you silently – in my heart."

He could hardly hear the last words, but he held her a little closer as he said,

"It is something you will have to forget. It was, of course, all Charlotte's doing and I guessed it as soon as I heard that you had been asked for by a gypsy woman."

"That was so – clever of you," she managed to say.

"I could only guess what had happened and I admit to being very anxious in case I was wrong and should have taken different steps to find you."

"But you found me," Serla sighed, "and I thought I might – never see you again."

He did not answer as he was wishing that he could punish Charlotte for her wicked plot to dispose of Serla.

He knew only too well, but he had no intention of telling Serla, what might have happened to her.

If they were the mercenary sort of gypsies who he suspected they were, they would have sold her to a bawdy house for a few pounds.

That would add to the money Charlotte had already given them.

Serla would have been doped and held captive until she could no longer understand what was happening to her.

Alternatively she might, as he had thought initially, have been dropped into a river or thrown into a ravine and she would never have been found.

It was attempted murder, but it was something that he could not prove. Nor had he any wish to do so, because if he did, it would involve Serla and himself.

He only thanked God more fervently than he had already that he could ever have been deceived by her.

Aloud he asked Serla,

"Are you quite comfortable? I am not going too fast for you?"

"Nothing matters except that you are here and I am not lying tied up in that caravan – and terrified."

"You must take care of yourself," the Marquis said. "I shall, of course, protect you, but never again, never – "

He paused as if to make his words more impressive as he finished.

" – must you follow a woman, who comes to the door to ask for your help."

"It is what very often – happened at home," Serla explained. "People would come to ask for Mama if they had cut their hand – or their children had taken a tumble or they were just feeling ill. It never entered my head – that the gypsy woman was dangerous."

"Well, in the future you must be more careful," the Marquis replied.

"I will do exactly – what you tell me," Serla said in a low voice.

She was resting her cheek against his coat.

She felt being so close to him with his arm around her was like being in Paradise.

'I love him, I love him,' she said to herself, 'but he must never know. His grandmother had warned me against falling in love with him, but how can I help it?'

The Marquis rode directly back over the fields to Darincourt Hall. It did not take as long as when he was going slowly and listening for the call of the owl.

When he and Serla saw the house in front of them, its lit windows beaming a welcome, the Marquis said,

"I think it would be a mistake to tell Grandmama what has happened."

"Of course," she replied. "It would only upset her."

"Then do slip upstairs and go to bed," he suggested. "If she is awake, I will tell her that I have just arrived back from London, but I expect she is asleep. I will tell Desbury that no one is to be aware of what has happened tonight."

"All that I can remember," Serla said very softly, "is that you came – when I called you."

The Marquis smiled.

As they reached the front door, in the light from the windows, he could see Serla very clearly.

She was looking, he thought, very lovely with her golden hair against his shoulder.

He was suddenly aware, and he had never thought of it before, that she had never been kissed.

He could not believe that she would have allowed Lord Charlton to kiss her on such a short acquaintance and she had said so often that she had met very few men.

He tried hard to remember when he had last kissed anyone who was young, so innocent and untouched, but he could not recall anyone but the sophisticated and flirtatious beauties he had been involved with.

Then he told himself that to kiss Serla, however, pleasant it might be, would be a mistake.

She had saved him from being married to Charlotte and that would have been a complete and utter disaster!

In return he now had to find a suitable husband for Serla, sometime in the future.

If she fell in love with him, it could present many difficulties.

So he must not kiss her even though he knew that it was something he wanted to do.

He drew in his horse by the front door and Serla lifted her head from his shoulder.

"You have brought me – home," she murmured.

"Safely," the Marquis said. "Now go upstairs, go to sleep and forget it ever happened."

For a moment she did not move from his arms.

"I just want to say thank you, but there are – no words."

She looked up at him.

He had a strange feeling that she wanted him to kiss her.

Then, as he told himself it was just his imagination, she slipped down from the saddle onto the ground.

Desbury was standing at the front door and as Serla ran up the steps he said,

"Are you all right, miss? It were a real shock when we found you'd disappeared."

"His Lordship found me," she answered, "and now I am going to bed."

She ran up the stairs without waiting for Desbury to say anything more.

She climbed into bed and cuddled down against the pillows.

She pretended to herself that she was still riding on the Marquis's saddle and his arm was round her.

'He saved me,' she told herself, 'and how could I ask for more than that?'

She knew, because she had been so close to him and so very near to his lips, that she did want more.

She had wanted, as she had never wanted anything in her whole life, that he should kiss her goodnight.

'I love him, I love him,' she was still whispering as she fell asleep.

*

The next morning Serla felt the reaction to all that she had been through.

She had hoped, before she finally fell asleep, that she might be able to ride early with the Marquis.

However it was almost ten o'clock before she woke up and then she still felt tired.

It was too much of an effort even to ring the bell to let her maid know that she was awake.

Instead she lay quietly in bed, thinking over what had happened and how lucky it was that the Marquis had been able to save her.

'He is so wonderful,' she told herself. 'What other man would have been clever enough to find me?'

Then, because she wanted to see him, she could not bear to waste time and forced herself to get up.

When she finally walked downstairs, it was to find that the Marquis had gone out and Desbury thought that he was riding over the estate.

Serla gave a deep sigh.

How could she have been so silly as to sleep and feel tired when she might be riding with the Marquis?

The Dowager came down for luncheon and was so delighted to find that the Marquis had returned.

Both he and Serla knew, as soon as they saw her that she had not been told about what had happened the night before.

The Marquis gave her a message from the Prince Regent and they talked about London during luncheon.

The Dowager had received a good number of letters thanking her for the ball and they had all said that it was the best one they had been to in years.

"You will have to think of something fantastic for your next effort, Grandmama," the Marquis pointed out.

"And you will both have to help me," she replied.

After luncheon, although she still felt rather tired, Serla did ride with the Marquis.

When they were away from the house, he asked,

"Are you all right? I thought that you might make some excuse to stay in bed today."

"I am all right. After all, when you were at war you could hardly take the day off after a battle and I am rather ashamed of not being up early to ride before breakfast."

"I missed you, but it was very sensible of you to stay where you were."

They rode on for a little while and then Serla said,

"You do not think that Charlotte – will try again?"

The Marquis shrugged his shoulders.

"I think it will be quite some time before she learns that her first effort has failed and anyway she will know that we are now on our guard and prepared for her."

"It frightens me," Serla shivered.

As she spoke, she felt that she wanted to put out her hand and hold onto the Marquis.

He turned his head to smile at her.

"You have been so brave. I cannot believe that you and I with our exceptional brains cannot defeat Charlotte, whatever horror she tries to torment us with."

"We ought – to be able to," Serla agreed.

At the same time she was frightened.

When they went back to the house there was a large pile of letters for the Marquis, which had been delivered by the postman and there was one letter for Serla.

When she picked it up, she realised at once who it was from and quickly hid it from the Marquis and it was only when she went to her room that she could open it.

It was, of course, from Lord Charlton.

"*Dearest, Beautiful Serla,*" he began.

"*I love you and I think I will always love you, but I have bad news.*

I told my mother what I felt about you and how I had asked you to run away with me and she was very upset.

She has not been very well for some time and I was ashamed of being so stupid as to confide in her without realising how much it would perturb her.

She knew your mother and the trouble there was when she ran away and so she has made me promise that I will not ask you to run away with me because it would affect the whole family.

I had to agree, but I don't know what else I can do to take you away from the Marquis.

I do so love you, Serla, and no one could be more beautiful or sweeter, but, as you will understand, I cannot make my mother unhappy.

So please forgive me and think about me as I shall be thinking about you.

David."

Serla read the letter through and could understand exactly what had happened.

Lord Charlton was still only a boy and very much a contrast to the Marquis who was definitely a man.

If she was in trouble she would not be able to rely on David, but the Marquis had proved himself, not once but twice when she was in danger.

'Perhaps he will not want me to leave for some time and then someone else will turn up,' she tried to tell herself.

But she knew what really terrified her was that she would have to leave the Marquis eventually.

When that did happen, she would leave her heart behind with him and life could never be the same again.

Because she felt that she might be late she hurriedly changed for dinner and went downstairs.

"You are early," the Marquis commented when she appeared. "Grandmama says that it is too much trouble to come down to dinner with us, so we are alone."

Serla was afraid that he would see in her eyes how much she loved him, so she looked away and then said,

"You promised to show me your secret passages."

"Of course, I did," the Marquis replied, "and, as a special treat, because you have been such a brave girl, I will show them to you now."

He walked towards the fireplace and, feeling along the wall beside it, he opened a panel.

Serla gave a little cry of excitement.

"Is there one in every room?" she asked.

"In quite a number," he answered. "Wherever they were, if the Protestants were told that the Catholics were coming they could then disappear and even if the Catholics searched the house they could not find them."

"They must have been exciting times," Serla said.

"The same happened later with the Roundheads and the Royalists," he went on. "I believe that my ancestors, who were Royalists, escaped death a dozen times when the Roundheads searched this house from top to bottom and they were hiding just the other side of the wall. Come and look."

He put out his hand and helped Serla through the secret panel and closed it behind them.

She found herself in a very narrow passage between the panelling and the wall. It was cleverly constructed with an aperture from which, while the sun was shining, there was enough light to see their way.

"It also brings in fresh air," the Marquis said, as Serla looked up at the light. "That was important if anyone had to stay in these passages for a long time."

They walked on a little further and came first to the Chapel. This was where the Clergy had held their Services without being detected.

There was a narrow altar built half into the wall with a beautiful golden cross above it and on one side there was a table and on it there were two large pistols.

"So they were armed!" Serla exclaimed.

"I think those were added in the Royalist days," the Marquis explained. "The experts who have seen the pistols claim that they were made at about that time."

They were large and rather heavy weapons and then Serla saw two smaller pistols lying beside them.

She looked at the Marquis for an explanation and he told her with a smile,

"They have been added by me. As you know, and we certainly proved the necessity of it last night, I made my grooms learn to shoot and also the footmen. There are so many valuables in this house, but, if the burglars do take us unawares, they are in for a big surprise!"

"So you have loaded pistols here ready to protect yourself and I suspect there are pistols in your writing desk and, of course, by your bed."

"I like to be forearmed and, as you saw last night, it is the man who is the strongest who wins the battle."

"I am very very grateful that you won mine," Serla sighed.

As if he felt a little embarrassed by her gratitude, the Marquis led her further on.

He showed her places where those who had to stay in the hidden passages for a long time could sleep.

They were almost like bunks on a ship and in one place there were four bunks rising one above another.

"Do you think that they really had to stay here for a long time?" Serla asked him.

"I believe one of my ancestors never dared to come out for three months because the Roundheads were very determined to shoot or hang him. Eventually they went away having been told by the household that he had gone abroad to join King Charles. Actually he remained here until the Restoration of the Monarchy."

"How fascinating," Serla enthused. "You must give me a book to read all about it."

"I will. Now it is about time for dinner, so I will take you back through my study."

He pressed a catch in the wall and, when it opened, Serla found herself beside the mantelpiece in the Marquis's study.

"There are more passages," he said, "which go as far as the dining room and one that goes out into the garden behind some shrubs, so that it is never seen."

"It is all so exciting," Serla said. "Thank you for letting me into your secret passages."

"They really are kept secret. None of the servants have any idea that they are here and only members of the family, which for the moment includes you, are allowed to know of their very existence, although they are mentioned in several history books of ancestral homes."

"I feel very privileged," Serla responded, "and, if I disappear again – you will know where I am!"

"It will certainly be easier to find you here than it was last night," the Marquis smiled.

He was thinking how he had trusted his instinct and once again it had not failed him.

Several times during the War he had saved his men by doing the unexpected and he had not even been certain himself whether he was doing right or wrong. But he had followed his instinct and it had not let him down.

As they walked towards the dining room, Serla was thinking that everything about the Marquis was exactly as it should be.

Who else could have such a reputation for gallantry and be recognised as one of the Heroes of the War?"

Who else had such a magnificent house and estate?

Who else had fantastic secret passages that were as intriguing as the history of the Darincourts themselves?

They reached the dining room and the Marquis sat down at the head of the table, which was weighed down with shining silver.

Serla could see his handsome features in a number of the pictures that decorated the walls. They were of the Earls who had lived here when the house was first built.

She was silent, thinking about him and she knew that his portrait would soon be added to those on the walls.

Later his son would be sitting as he was now at the head of the table.

But Serla came up against an unjumpable fence.

She remembered that the Marquis was determined, after what Charlotte had done to him, never to be married.

'But he must be, he must carry on the name of the family and this house,' she told herself.

As she thought how wrong it would be if he refused to do so, her eyes met his.

As they gazed at each other, she was aware that the Marquis was reading her thoughts.

It was just as if Charlotte was there beside them.

She was jeering at him for having been deceived by her.

Serla was aware that he could see Charlotte just as she could.

She knew, without his saying it aloud, that he was repeating over and over in his mind.

"No! No! *No!*"

CHAPTER SEVEN

The Marquis laughed a lot over dinner.

After it was over they moved to his study to see the paintings that they had been talking about. They had been painted by the great equestrian artist, Stubbs, and Serla was particularly interested in them.

Her father had one of his earliest paintings and had longed to buy more.

"There are two more upstairs in the Picture Gallery that you have not yet seen," the Marquis said, "and I agree with your father that no one managed to make his horses quite so real as Stubbs."

They talked for a while and then the Marquis said,

"I think that you are tired and should retire. I have just a few letters to write and then I shall go to bed too. Let's hope it will be peaceful tonight."

"I hope so too," Serla smiled.

She knew that she was tired, but did not want to leave the Marquis.

He walked to the door to open it for her and, as she looked up at him, he thought again how lovely she was.

It would be delightful to kiss her goodnight.

Almost abruptly, because of the feelings that she was arousing within him, he said again 'good night.'

Then he closed the door and Serla walked through the hall and saw that the night-footman had come on duty.

He had a cushioned armchair to sit in and she knew that, as soon as everyone had gone to bed, he too would sleep peacefully until the morning.

"Goodnight, James," she called as she passed him.

"Goodnight, miss," James replied.

Serla then walked slowly up the stairs to her room.

She undressed and put on her nightgown and it was then that she remembered that she had not said 'goodnight' to the Dowager.

It was stupid of her to have forgotten, but she had, however, been deep in thought as she had come upstairs.

She was determined that she would ride early with the Marquis tomorrow morning and she had taken out her riding habit and boots so that she could dress quickly.

She walked across the corridor and knocked on the door of the Dowager's bedroom.

Serla heard her call out 'come in' and entered.

*

When Serla had left the study, the Marquis went to his writing table as there was a large pile of letters that his secretary had left for him to sign.

Mr. Simpkins was well versed in what he should and should not open and the Marquis had never bothered with bills, letters from Councils or requests for money.

Mr. Simpkins coped with all these and he was very adroit in detecting those which were not his concern.

Granted, as the Marquis noticed now, most of these were on pretty coloured writing paper, most scented with an exotic perfume.

The Marquis glanced at them and then pushed them to one side as he recognised that they would all be full of reproaches because he had become engaged to be married.

At the same time the writer would invariably make a suggestion where they could meet without her husband or anyone else being aware of it.

'They bore me,' the Marquis told himself and yet he did not want to probe too deeply into the reason why they did.

There was a letter from the Secretary of State for War which he had to read and one he had to write to the Prime Minister to thank him for his hospitality.

When he had done this, he decided to go to bed and he shut the drawers in his desk and closed his blotter.

As he did so, the door of the study opened and the night-footman announced,

"Two gentlemen from the War Office to see you, my Lord."

The Marquis looked up in surprise and then, as two men came into the room, he rose to his feet.

He wondered what had happened that they should come to see him so late at night.

He reached the centre of the room by the time they joined him and the door closed behind them.

Then to his astonishment the two men pulled pistols from their pockets and pointed them at him.

The long years of being confronted by the enemy in Spain made the Marquis keep his head and his self-control.

Without moving and without flickering an eyelid, he asked quite calmly,

"Now what is all this about?"

"We've come, my Lord," one of the men replied, "to ask you politely to hand over the Darincourt jewellery."

The Marquis raised his eyebrows.

"The Darincourt jewellery?" he repeated. "Just why should you want that?"

The man smiled unpleasantly.

"I'm sure Your Lordship knows the answer to that question and we requires it now and at once."

"Can you give me any good reason why I should hand it to you?" the Marquis asked quietly.

"Because," the man replied, "there be four of us all fully armed and you'll find it ever so uncomfortable to say the least of it if you prefer to fight us."

"I would certainly not do anything so foolish," the Marquis said loftily.

He was playing for time and wondering frantically how he could reach his pistol. It was in the drawer of the writing desk that he had just closed.

He was aware, however, that the man had implied that there were two fellow conspirators in the hall and there was no one except for the night-footman in this part of the house at this time of night.

"I should be interested," the Marquis said aloud, "to know why you are so anxious to steal the family jewels when there are so many other things in this house that you might prefer. And who is it who wishes to wear them?"

He knew the answer only too clearly.

He had to acknowledge, although it was infuriating to do so, that Charlotte had again caught him unawares.

Far too late he realised that having, as she thought, disposed of Serla, she was determined that he too should suffer for what he had done to her.

There was no woman in all of the *Beau Monde* who did not covet the Darincourt jewels and the Marquis knew that Charlotte wanted them as so many women had done before her.

She had often talked about them and had eulogised about how magnificent the tiara was and how exquisite the rubies, emeralds and sapphires would look on anyone with a white skin.

She was, of course, meaning herself.

Skilfully he had managed to avoid, as another man might not have done, letting her put them on.

He had on several nights when she came to stay at Darincourt made an excuse not to open the safes.

He knew now what would be the greatest triumph of Charlotte's life, she would steal the sublime Darincourt jewels from him and keep them for herself.

She would not, of course, be able to wear them in public as they would be easily recognised.

However, any jeweller could change the settings of the diamonds and the other precious stones and it would be impossible to prove in a Law Court where they had come from.

The very idea of Charlotte possessing anything so precious was infuriating as the jewels had been in his family for generations and the Marquis felt as if he would fight the whole world rather than lose them.

He was, however, wise enough to know that he was at a great disadvantage. It would require all his wits and courage to save himself from the humiliation of handing over the jewels.

Moving a few steps towards the fireplace, he said,

"Now let's talk it over sensibly. You cannot really mean to deprive me of the jewels which have been in the Darincourt family for over five hundred years."

"That's what we've come to do," the man who had been speaking before replied. "And the sooner we gets down to business, my Lord, the better."

Looking at him, the Marquis thought that he was a superior type of criminal.

Such men were far more dangerous than those who were rough and coarse and he obviously had brains and a shrewd look about him that was echoed by his companion.

That there were four men made it seem completely impossible for the Marquis to resist them in any way.

He managed to walk over to the mantelpiece with their pistols still pointing at him and then he said,

"Now, I think you must know or suspect that these jewels are not kept all together in one place. There are several safes and, since I have a large quantity of jewellery, what I suggest is you tell me exactly what you require. I will then know which safe to open and that will save time."

"We're in no particular hurry, my Lord," the man said with a smirk. "And, of course, a jewel is always a jewel whether it be the one we are looking for or perhaps one which is better."

"I still think it would be easier if I know exactly what you require," the Marquis replied. "Or shall I say the lady you are taking all this trouble over knows which jewel will accentuate her beauty better than another."

The man gave an amused laugh and sneered,

"Now come on, my Lord. We've got you up against the wall, so to speak, and there's nothing you can do about it. Hand them all over and we'll not trouble you anymore."

"It is not quite as easy as that. For one thing, I am trying to remember where the keys are kept and I am sure that you have no wish for me to arouse the household."

"You find the keys on your own," the man replied, "or we'll make it unpleasant for anyone who helps you."

"Frankly, that is just what frightens me. Now give me a moment to think things out. As, of course, you are well aware, I have been abroad for a long time and much of what happens in this house is new to me."

"According to the newspapers your grandmother was wearing the tiara two nights ago in London. So if you don't know where it be, we can wake her up and ask her."

It was a threat, as the Marquis was well aware.

However, he deliberately ignored it and sat down in a chair by the side of the fireplace.

"Now while I am thinking," he said, "why not help yourselves to a drink? You must have come a long way. On the grog table over there, there is everything that you might fancy while I try to sort this matter out."

The two men hesitated and then, as if temptation was too great, one said,

"Well, we might just as well accept your offer, but don't play any tricks while we're drinking your health."

The Marquis chuckled.

"I am not so stupid as to do that. Help yourselves, only leave just one for me when you are gone. I am quite certain that I shall need a drink and a strong one!"

The way he spoke made the men laugh, but weakly as if they thought he might be tricking them in some way.

They walked towards the grog table and they kept looking back to make quite sure that he was not moving.

Or had managed in some way that they were not aware of to procure a weapon of some kind.

The Marquis was, however, just lounging back in the armchair. It was as if he was entirely at ease, with one hand lying on the arm of the chair, the other on his knee.

He was actually wondering if by some miracle he could open the secret panel and then, while the two men were drinking, he would be able to disappear inside it.

It was, he reflected, the only chance that he had to prevent them carrying off the Darincourt jewels.

Even so, he was afraid that if he made the slightest noise they would turn and shoot him with their pistols.

He was watching as one man very carefully poured champagne that was standing in an ice-cooler into a glass.

He was using only his right hand with his left still clutching his pistol. The other man, who had picked up the decanter of port, was doing the same thing.

It was then, while the Marquis was wondering if he dare attempt to open the secret panel, that he heard a very slight click.

*

Serla stayed talking to the Dowager for a little time and then she said,

"You must go to sleep, Grandmama, and me too."

"You looked rather tired last night, my dear, I was glad you did not go riding this morning."

"I overslept, but I shall tomorrow. I missed riding one of your grandson's magnificent new horses and will not be so silly another day."

"There is no hurry," the Dowager said, "the horses will be there for a long time."

"But I may not," she sighed beneath her breath.

The Dowager put out her hand.

"I want you to stay as long as you can," she said. "I love having you and I know that Clive does as well, even though he may not say so."

"I expect he will get tired of me just as he tired of those other beautiful ladies."

"I am praying – praying every night that he will not do so," the Dowager replied.

Serla looked surprised and then she answered,

"That is very sweet of you. I love being here and I love you."

She nearly added,

'And I love your grandson,' but knew that it was something that she should not say.

Yet she guessed that the Dowager was aware of it and she put out her hand and laid it on Serla's.

"I like to think, my dear, that my prayers are always answered. I know that God hears them and He has been very kind to me in the past."

Serla bent forward and kissed her cheek.

"I am praying too."

She wanted to tell the Dowager how she had prayed last night and how the Marquis had found her and so her prayers had been answered.

But he had said that if his grandmother learned of what had happened she would be most upset and that was something he did not want.

'He is so very kind and considerate,' Serla thought. 'Yet he will not make his grandmother happy by giving her the one thing she really wants, which is an heir.'

Aloud she said,

"Good night, Grandmama, and, when I get to my bedroom, I shall pray exactly as you have told me to."

"And I shall be praying here and I am quite certain that your prayers and mine will fly straight up to Heaven."

Serla kissed her again and walked towards the door and as she reached it she looked back.

She thought how attractive the Dowager looked in the candlelight and she could understand any man loving someone who was so beautiful, whatever age she might be.

Serla closed the door.

And she was walking along the landing to her room when she heard the sound of wheels outside the front door.

She stopped, wondering who it could possibly be at this time of night.

The night-footman opened the front door and Serla could see that there were four men outside.

She could not imagine who they could be and why were they calling on the Marquis so late?

Then she heard one of the men say,

"We wish to speak to the Marquis of Darincourt."

As he spoke, the four men moved into the hall.

To Serla they all looked very much alike, but there seemed something strange about their appearance and she could not think what it was.

They did not look like businessmen and they were definitely not gentlemen.

"His Lordship's in the study," the footman said.

He spoke as if he was a little uncertain of what he should do.

"Take us to him," the man ordered.

"If you'll come this way, sir," the footman replied.

The man took a step forward and then he looked back at the two men behind him.

"Stay here," he told them, "until I want you."

They obeyed him without speaking and then they sat down one on each side of the hall.

The footman and the other two disappeared into the corridor which led to the study.

As they did so Serla saw one of the men open his coat and look down, as if making sure that something was there.

She then saw what he was looking at was a pistol.

It was then she realised with a considerable shock that the Marquis was in danger.

The four men were armed and he was alone in his study. All the servants, apart from the night-footman, were in another part of the house.

Without thinking, just following her instinct as the Marquis would have done, she ran into the boudoir.

She felt for the catch which opened the secret panel beside the fireplace.

The Marquis, she remembered, had said that most of the State rooms were connected with the passage on the ground floor they had walked down this morning.

As the panel opened silently, she knew that she had not been mistaken.

She groped her way down some steps and then she was in the secret passage that the Marquis had shown her.

There was a faint light from the moon and the stars for her to find the way.

Serla started to move as fast as she could towards the little Chapel.

As she reached the altar she remembered the pistols that had been on the table beside it.

The old ones, which were not loaded and the two modern ones which were.

She then picked the loaded pistols up and carried them carefully in case she should pull the trigger by mistake.

It was not far to the study and, when she reached it, she could see the door quite clearly.

She could also hear voices.

The Marquis was talking to the two men, who had been shown into the room by the footman.

She heard him saying that they might like a drink while he thought about what he should do. Then she heard one of the men threatening him if he attempted to escape.

Suddenly Serla saw that there was a small hole in the panel and through it she could see into the study.

It was so small that she was sure that it could not be seen from the other side and by pressing her eye against it she could see the two men walking towards the grog table.

They were quickly out of sight as the mantelpiece intervened.

It was then she realised that straight in front of her the Marquis was sitting in an armchair. She had, when she had first looked, only seen the room above his head and the men walking towards the corner.

Nor was she aware that, because the Marquis had been working at his writing desk, the candles in the other part of the room had not been lit.

So he was in a poor light and it was impossible to see clearly the chair where he was seated.

That also meant that the secret panel itself was in semi-darkness.

Then there was the chink of glasses.

Very very cautiously Serla opened the door.

She prayed that the men would be too concerned with what they were doing to notice her.

Very gently she pressed one of the pistols into the Marquis's hand as it lay on the arm of the chair.

He took it and at once dropped his arm and it would be impossible for the men drinking to realise that he was now holding something in his hand.

The man who had poured out the port now lifted up his glass.

"I drink your health, my Lord," he said, "and I'll drink it again when I leaves here with the goods you're going to give me."

The other man then spoke for the first time,

"You're missing a real treat. This here bubbly's first rate and you're a fool to prefer that red muck."

He spoke in a coarse common way and the man with the glass of port turned on him almost angrily,

"My taste's as good as yours – " he began to say.

He turned his head as he spoke.

As he did so, the Marquis, with the expertise of a sportsman, shot him through the wrist.

Even as he did so Serla pushed her way through the secret door and shot the other man in the right shoulder.

The two reports rang out and seemed to echo round the room.

The men who were shot screamed and fell onto the floor and they dropped both their glasses and their pistols.

With the quickness that the Marquis had learned on the battlefield, he sprang out of his chair.

He pushed Serla back through the secret panel and followed her and, when they were both inside, he shut the panel firmly.

Now they could only hear the men groaning.

The Marquis did not say a word, he just took Serla by the hand and pulled her along the secret passage.

When they reached the Chapel, he took the pistol from her and put it back on the table she had taken it from.

Then he pulled her along with him until they had reached the steps that led up to the boudoir.

"You were very brave, so wonderful and you saved me," he breathed at last.

"What are you going to do?" Serla asked. "There are two other men – in the hall."

"I know," the Marquis answered. "I will deal with them and there will be no problem, thanks to you."

"Please, please be – careful," she said incoherently.

She did not want him to leave her, but she knew that he would have to go.

Without thinking she put out her arms as if to hold onto him.

The Marquis pulled her against him and then his lips were on hers.

He kissed her fiercely and possessively.

Then, almost before she could grasp the wonder and thrill of it, he set her free and ordered her gently,

"Go to your bedroom, Serla, and lock the door."

Then he was gone.

She could only hear the sound of his footsteps as he ran along the passage towards the dining room.

She knew at once that he had gone to rouse the other footmen who were sleeping on the ground floor.

She remembered that they had all learned to shoot and now the Marquis was no longer alone, having his men to support him.

For a moment it was impossible to move and Serla felt as if her head was whirling.

The tension she had felt when she had opened the secret panel was still making it hard to breathe. Yet the Marquis was now safe.

She had saved him, just as he had saved her last night.

Slowly, because she knew that she must obey him, she climbed up the small steps which led to her boudoir.

The panel at the top was ajar and she slipped into the room, feeling as if a thousand things had happened since she had left it.

How was it possible that those four men had come fully armed to demand something from the Marquis that he had no wish to give them.

As she thought about it, she guessed what they had wanted, but she might be wrong.

She was virtually certain that Charlotte in her desire to hurt the Marquis had sent the men to steal the Darincourt jewels.

The newspapers had all described how magnificent they were when the Dowager had worn them at her ball and there had been almost as much written about the jewels as the ball itself.

That, Serla said to herself, was what they had come for and that was why the Marquis had kissed her because she had saved them for him.

She could still feel the insistence of his lips on hers.

It was the most wonderful feeling that she had ever known.

At the same time she could not pretend that it was a kiss of love rather than one of gratitude.

Perhaps too, she thought, it was a kiss of relief that the jewels were now safe, safe for the wife he would one day take for himself.

Equally he had kissed her.

'He has kissed me! He has kissed me!' Serla said in her heart. 'When I leave, I shall have that to remember.'

She thought that the thrill that had run through her had been like a streak of forked lightening. Or was it the moonlight that had made it possible for her to find her way down the secret passage?

In her bedroom she thought that if she was sensible she would do what the Marquis had told her and go to bed.

It could be hours before he came to tell her that it was all over.

Then suddenly she was afraid.

He should have collected the footmen by now.

They should be approaching, perhaps furtively, the two men sitting in the hall.

If she heard shots, what should she do?

She realised that the Marquis did not wish her to be involved in what was happening.

Yet he was in danger and she felt that she must be near to him. Perhaps she would be able to help him again.

He had taken the pistol from her and she wished now that she had held onto it.

If she saw someone threatening him, she could have shot them from the top of the stairs as she had shot the man in the study.

She went to the door of her bedroom and listened, but she could not hear anything.

Were the two men in the hall still sitting there?

Surely they, if no one else, would have heard the reports from the pistol shots in the study.

It was all terrifying.

Because she did not know what was happening, she could only imagine the worst.

'Save him. Oh, please God save him,' she prayed. 'He must not be injured, please, please keep him safe.'

Because she could not keep still, she walked to the window. Everything in the garden was quiet and peaceful.

The moon turned everything to silver and the stars were twinkling above the trees.

'I must know if he is safe,' Serla decided.

As she did so she heard the door open behind her.

She turned round and saw the Marquis silhouetted against the light in the passage.

She gave a cry of sheer relief and ran towards him and threw herself against him saying incoherently,

"You are – safe, they did not hurt you, you are – all right?"

The Marquis pulled her against him.

Then he was kissing her, not fiercely as he had done before, but possessively, as if she was something that he had wanted for a long time and had found it at last.

Serla felt as if the doors of Paradise had opened and she could hear the angels singing.

The Marquis's kisses and the strength of his arms made thrill after thrill run through her.

She felt as if she had reached Heaven and they were both part of it.

It was a long while before the Marquis raised his head and she could stammer,

"You are – all right? They have not – hurt you? I was so – frightened."

"I am perfectly all right," he answered. "How could you have been so clever, my darling, to save me when I thought that I would have to give them what they wanted?"

"What did they – want?" Serla asked.

"The family jewels," he replied. "It was Charlotte's determination to hurt me and she would have succeeded if you had not come to my rescue."

He did not wait for Serla to answer him and instead he kissed her again, holding her so close that she felt as if her body melted into his.

They were no longer two people but one.

Only when he raised his head again did Serla say as if she could not help it,

"I love you, I love you."

"And I love you," the Marquis said. "I have fought against it for days or what seems like years and I cannot go on fighting. The battle of love is over. I love you, my darling, and I know that I cannot live without you."

Serla made a sound which was half a sob.

"I don't believe – I am hearing this," she sighed.

"Then I will say it again. I love you and the sooner we are married the safer we will be."

Serla gave a cry of horror.

"You mean Charlotte will try again?"

"Actually," the Marquis answered, "I think that will be impossible for her."

"But why?" Serla asked.

The Marquis picked her up in his arms and carried her to the bed. He put her down so that she was lying against the pillows and then he said,

"We can hardly go on standing in the door when I have so much to say and so many kisses to give you."

"Oh, Clive, is it really true that you love me?" Serla asked.

"It will take a whole lifetime for me to tell you how much," he replied. "But first I want to tell you what has happened."

Serla put out her hand to hold onto him as she was afraid of what she might hear, but he said quietly,

"It is all over. When you were clever enough, my darling, to give me the pistol and I shot one man and you shot the other one, as I anticipated the two men who were waiting in the hall came rushing into the room."

"If you had stayed – they might have shot you," Serla said in a frightened voice.

"Of course they would, which was why I hurried you away. What I did not expect was that when they saw their fellow criminals writhing on the floor they ran away and left them."

"Left them?"

"According to the footman, they ran through the hall without stopping, jumped into the post chaise that they had come in and drove away."

"I can hardly believe it," Serla sighed.

"It is true. When I roused the footman and we went into the hall with more weapons to defend ourselves with, it was to find the two men had gone and the other two we had left in the study were groaning on over their wounds."

"So what did you do?" Serla asked.

"They have been locked up and tomorrow they will be handed over to the Police, who will take them before the Magistrates. They will be charged with attempted burglary and the carrying of firearms, both of which are punishable by many years imprisonment."

"Well, that is two of them – out of the way," Serla said. "What about the others?"

"I doubt if they will come back," the Marquis said, "but you must understand, darling, that the two wounded men have given us a weapon which will silence Charlotte and make her behave properly in the future."

Serla looked at him in surprise.

"How can that be?" she asked.

"I shall inform her that they have revealed to me who sent them to steal the Darincourt jewellery. I shall tell her that, if she threatens you or me again in any way, I will denounce her to the Court and she will doubtless be sent to prison as well as the two men carrying out her orders."

Serla looked relieved.

"I don't think she will try again – to hurt you after that."

"I shall also say that the gypsies told me that it was she who had paid them to abduct you. With two such possible charges against her there is nothing that Charlotte can do but behave herself."

"She should be grateful that you are so merciful,"

"I do *not* wish your name to be dragged through the mud," the Marquis said, "and my family would be shocked if anything defamatory was said of the new Marchioness of Darincourt."

He bent forward as he spoke and Serla put her arms round his neck.

"Are you really and truly – asking me to marry – you?" she quavered.

The Marquis smiled.

"I am not asking you, I am telling you that we are going to be married as quickly as is possible so that I can look after you and protect you. Not only by day but also by night."

"It's too good – to be true," she murmured.

"I will make it all come true. And you know that Grandmama will be delighted."

"She has been praying that this would happen and now she will know that her prayers have been answered."

She looked at the Marquis and then, hiding her face against his neck, she added a little shyly,

"And so will – mine."

"I was determined not to let you fall in love with me," the Marquis pointed out.

"But how could I help it," she said. "When you are so handsome – so marvellous and so brave?"

"That is how I want you to think about me. At the same time, my darling, I think we will be very happy. I have no wish to spend any more time in London, but here in Darincourt with our horses and, of course, our children."

Serla gave a little laugh.

"It is what they all wanted and what you refused."

"That was because I had not met you," the Marquis answered. "Actually as soon as I saw you I knew that you were different from anyone I had ever known. Now you have crept into my heart and possessed it and I shall never look at another woman because you are everything that is perfect."

Serla gave a little cry and then she admitted,

"I was just thinking that when you decided you no longer wanted to pretend that I was your fiancée, I would perhaps be able to stay with you as your Cyprian."

He stared at her and she hid her face against him.

"Grandmama has told me what they really are, but I thought as you had no wish to be married I would be very happy if I could just be with you as I love you so much."

For a second he drew in his breath and closed his eyes as he could hardly believe what he had just heard.

Yet he knew that he had found what he wanted.

A woman who loved him, not for his title but for himself.

A woman who was prepared, so long as she could be with him, to sacrifice everything she believed was right rather than lose his love.

He put his arms round her and held her very close.

"I just love you and adore you. I also worship you because you are good and because you pray for what you want. I swear to you, my darling, when we are married I will never let anything spoil you and you will never do anything that is wrong or what in your innermost heart you know is wicked."

Serla did not really understand.

At the same time, because the Marquis's voice was deep and sincere, she felt very moved.

"I love you," she said. "I love you so much you fill my whole world and there is no one else but you."

"That is what it will always be," he smiled.

Then he was kissing her again.

Kissing her until Serla felt that he was carrying her up into the sky.

They were part of the moonlight and the stars.

There was no more danger or fear or misery, just love.

A love that she had prayed for and which God had given them.

A love that came from Heaven and filled Clive's heart and hers and made them both part of the Divine.

Made in the USA
Monee, IL
13 April 2023

31411761R00095